THE RUMMY KID GOES HOME

The Rummy Kid

Goes Home ‿‿‿‿ and
Other Stories of the Southwest

BY ROSS SANTEE

with illustrations by the author

HASTINGS HOUSE, *Publishers* • NEW YORK

For Zilch and Jonnie

With the exception of "The Ring" and "The Orchard," here published for the first time, the stories in this book originally appeared in various magazines. *Collier's*: "Water" and "With Bated Breath." *Red Book*: "The Letter," "Wolf Call," "No Bracelets," "The Goat," "Lower Trail" and "One of the Outfit." *Country Home*: "Old Hand," "Tin Horn," "The Rummy Kid Goes Home" and "Man and Horse." *Farm and Fireside*: "A Cowpuncher's Letters from Hollywood." *Cavalcade*: "Old Jim Newton's Boy" (under the title "Riding Old Hellcat").

CONTENTS

WATER

SMITH dug out the spring while I fought the cattle back with a shovel. They were crazy for water. They had upset the trough. It was dry as a bone and they had tromped the pipe into the mud. There was a big steer in the bunch that had showed his hocks to my pony several times on Mescal Mountain. He was as wild as a black-tailed buck. Now his sunken eyes burned like live coals. I had to bat him twice on the nose with the shovel.

We set the trough in place and Smith cleaned out the pipe with a wire. There was only a trickle of water. He ran the wire through the pipe again — there was only a little trickle. Smith went kind of crazy then. He picked up a shovel and throwed it as far as he could. He said he didn't give a goddam if it ever rained. He laughed and cursed.

Then he went and got his pony. He didn't speak all the way to the ranch. I didn't say anything either. There wasn't anything to say with Mud Springs dry. It was all over. The oufit was blowed and broke.

It was tough on Smith. It was tough on his wife too. I was thinking of her as we rode to the ranch. Only the day before I'd come in ahead of Smith and found her kneeling on the ranch-house porch.

"God, give us rain," she says.

I don't know how she stood it as long as she did with the cattle bawling for water. They bawled all day. They bawled all night. It was a never ending sound. It was getting on me so I dreaded to come in nights. Even in the ranch house it was always in your ears.

Supper was waiting when Smith and me got in that night. His wife was pleasant as usual. And Smith was apparently over that spell of his at the spring. It was when she fetched the light that I noticed how old an' tired she was. Then I looked at Smith. He had aged ten years that day.

I noticed she didn't touch her food nor take a sip of coffee. Once way back when it started she had said it was all she could do to get it down when she thought of the thirsty cattle.

Nobody spoke. Outside the cattle bawled for water. Her eyes were on Smith's face. He wasn't eating either. Finally he pushed his plate aside.

"I guess you know," he says.

She nodded her head. When she spoke her voice was firm. "I know," she says, "Mud Springs went dry today."

Something pinched me in the throat when the woman smiled an' I walked outside the house. I knew they wanted to be alone.

Some thunderheads were hanging low over Mescal Rim. Once in the long ago it had been a sign of rain. But with tomorrow's blazing sun they would disappear again. A full moon was rising over Turnbull Peak. I had watched a full moon rise two years ago

from the same place on the ranch-house porch the night I came to work for Smith.

It was a regular cow spread then with fat ponies to ride and fat cattle. There had been good rains the year I come. There was plenty of feed and water. The big flats were covered with fillaree where the cattle grazed knee-deep. There was gramma on every hill. There wasn't an outfit in Arizona any better fixed for water.

I had often heard the woman speak of how they started out over twenty years before. She was teaching school. She had met Smith at a dance one night when he was a wild young puncher breaking horses at the Circles. Smith started to save his wages then an' he kept away from town. It was four years later that she put her money in with his and they bought a little remnant of cattle.

Smith had built the little house himself and he had put in all the corrals. Often she had held the lantern when he worked on them at night. There had been her little garden and an orchard.

Like all cow folks in Arizona they had had their ups and downs. There had been wet years and dry. They had owed the bank at different times but they always had paid out. They had watched the little remnant grow until they owned five thousand head. Then the drought. Now there wasn't half that many.

With rain the outfit could pull through even now. The cattle could live on browse and buck brush if only they had water. Even now there was plenty of feed way back in the hills if it rained an' put out water.

Thinking back it was hard to remember when Smith or I had used a rope or branding iron. We rode with picks and shovels digging out the springs and water holes. For weeks and months the thunderheads had come each day to mock us in the sky. But somehow there was always hope until Mud Springs went dry.

Their light still showed when I unrolled my bedroll on the porch. It didn't seem as if I'd been asleep. But it was the patter on the roof that woke me up at daybreak. The sky was dark and overcast. Mescal Rim was hid. The patter stopped and then it came, it came in driving torrents.

I could hear the folks inside as I pulled on my boots. I guess I acted funny. I didn't remember that I yelled. Later Smith said it was the first time he ever saw a cowboy drunk on nothing except water.

But I remember the woman kneeling in the rain and Smith, his head thrown back, the water streaming from his face, both hands stretched toward the sky.

And still it came. It was noon when we thought of breakfast. We laughed and talked all through the meal. We ate with the rain still pelting on the roof without any sign of a let-up.

The three of us sat late that night, it was pleasant on the porch. We sat and listened to the rain. And for the first time in the long, cruel months the bawling cattle were quiet.

It was just before they went inside Smith turned to me and spoke.

"Yesterday at the spring," he said, "I didn't mean that — what I said about it never raining."

THE LETTER

I T wasn't until Jim was asleep and the doctor had gone that Judy thought of her unfinished letter. As she sank into the rawhide-bottom chair the letter lay before her on the kitchen table. It all seemed ages ago; yet she had started it only that morning. She had been at the table when she heard the horse coming in.

At the first sound of the drumming hoofs she had run to the door. Who could be coming so fast? As long as she lived she would never forget the stark terror she felt at sight of the empty saddle. The big gray horse was Jim's. It was Pilot coming into the ranch from Red Mesa, coming in on the dead run.

Some things would always be hazy to Judy, others crystal clear. The deep gash in the cantle, the dirt on the horn showed that Pilot had fallen; the big gray horse had been down. She didn't remember mounting, how Pilot had snorted in fear or how she had crowded him against the corral fence so the big horse couldn't lunge and pull away as she swung up on him. Yet she remembered meeting Old Blaze, the horse she usually rode, coming into the ranch for water and how the old pony had pulled aside an' gazed wide-eyed as Pilot went thundering past. They were halfway to Red Mesa then. That was where she had found him. She was praying

13

aloud with his head in her lap when Jim finally opened his eyes.

When his head had cleared he had managed to crawl to a big flat rock. Pilot must have understood. He shook like a leaf as she held his head but he had made no move until Jim had eased down into the saddle.

She knew each breath had been torture as she walked and led the big horse. At first Jim had tried to talk: he had been running a "slick ear" when Pilot fell; the horse had rolled over him. "You've been holdin' out on me — that goes for Pilot too — couldn't hang a nosebag on him, afraid to go near his head!"

She had tried to answer in kind. "Anyone can ride your old gray horse, you've been kidding yourself all the time."

It was like him to rib her about stealing his horse. She knew the pride that he felt. No one ever rode Pilot but him; Pilot was his one-man horse.

The last mile, would it ever end? His eyes closed, he swayed drunkenly in the saddle and the knuckles of his hands were white as he gripped the saddle horn. Each time she had wanted to stop so he could rest — "Keep goin'," was all he said. At the ranch-house door he had slid from the horse; she had managed to break his fall. How she had managed to get him into the house and onto the bed Judy would never know.

All she recalled of the nine-mile ride to the telephone at the Ranger Station had been the sound of the doctor's voice and how Pilot's heart had pounded against her knee on the ride back to the ranch. She had remembered what Jim once said in the long, long ago:

"Reckon I like him because of his heart, he'll never quit on you!"

Now the broken ribs were taped. The doctor had said that the break in the leg was clean. "He's full of dope but he'll sleep tonight; try to get some yourself, my dear, I'll look in sometime tomorrow. He's going to be all right."

Never before had she been so tired. Sleep! It was out of the question. She was as wide awake as she was when she sat up at night waiting for him to come in. Outside a calf bawled for its mammy. It was deathly still in the house. She was conscious of the tick of the clock and the sound of his heavy breathing. As she dimmed the little coal-oil lamp she was conscious that a rising moon was flooding the rangeland with light. As she walked to the room and sat by his bed a coyote barked from the shadows. Through the window the moonlight streamed over the foot of the bed and made a bright patch on the floor. The moon had been full and riding high the first night she had come to the ranch. It was less than a year, yet it was ages ago.

It had been her first trip West. They had driven in from the dude ranch in the desert hills to the rodeo in Phoenix. He had tied a calf in front of their box. Someone had spoken to him. He had looked up into the box and smiled. She knew that she wanted him then.

She had stood and cheered each bronc rider in turn until he came out of the chute. She didn't know why she was quiet then, why she didn't move from her seat. The only emotion she had felt was relief when the ride was over, relief that he wasn't hurt.

They had met at a party in town that night. A week later they had been married. Aunt Susan, of course, had fainted the night she had called New York. Later Dad admitted to her that her call had upset him too. And he added with one of his wry smiles that only a bottle of spirits had kept him on his feet. But he had flown out for the wedding and caught a plane going East that night.

They had driven him out to the airport in a loaded truck with Pilot in a trailer behind. They were to start for the ranch when the plane left. Judy remembered the pride she had felt as she walked between the two men. Her big cowpuncher in cowboy togs, her Dad in his tailored clothes.

"I know you will take good care of her, Jim." Dad had smiled as he shook Jim's hand.

Jim's face had been deadly serious. "By God, I aim to," he said.

Judy knew Dad liked him but she was grateful for what he said. As he kissed her good-by he had whispered, "Be happy, my dear, your mother would have adored him."

Jim had spoken with pride of the cattle and horses. The house wasn't much, he had said, and the long, low unpainted affair had been a shock to her. Bedrolls, guns in a corner, a sack full of dirty clothes, slickers, chaps, old boots and big hats, a saddle that lay on the floor. Horse gear of every kind covered the walls and floor. What most of it was used for she didn't know or care. She realized she had moved into a world entirely strange, yet nothing really mattered then. She was so deeply in love she would have lived with him in a tepee.

She had thought, of course, that she would ride with him. She had soon learned there were no bridle paths here or dudes who went out on a string. Jim had

got up two old gentle ponies. They still rode to the Ranger Station together when he had business that way, and up to the old prospector's camp. She usually stopped and had a visit with old Mr. Smith while Jim went on to the mountain. There was the four-mile ride to the mailbox and back. She usually found a letter from Dad, he seldom missed a day. But it hadn't taken her long to find out that when there was any real work to be done out on the range she was only in Jim's way.

Dad sent her all the latest books. Some of her old favorite prints now hung on the ranch-house walls. With curtains and Navajo rugs on the floor the place was really snug. Yet she had come to resent it more and more since it had come to be her world.

Her first garden had been a mess. The canning had been worse, if possible. She had insisted that Jim get some chickens too. Then one night when he was

away she had forgot to shut the fool things up. Coyotes got most of them. The milk cow had been her idea too, the only one that turned out right. She was proud she could really milk and she really felt an affection for the cow. It was the only animal on the ranch that didn't seem to resent her.

The horses were tolerant enough to let her hang a nosebag on them when Jim was away from the ranch. Pilot alone had rebelled. He had snorted and struck with both forefeet when she went near his head. There was no love lost either as far as she was concerned. She had never admitted it to Jim but deep down in her heart Judy thought she knew the answer; the horses all resented her because she was afraid of them.

The punchers, Jim's friends who came to the ranch, had been a breed she didn't know. They lived in a world apart from her. It was Jim's world too and they spoke another language. "Slickears, sleepers, lati-goes, orejanos" had meant nothing, they were only so many strange words. She had soon learned to wait until she and Jim were alone before she asked her questions.

There had been the night when Skeeter and Jim were talking of quarter horses. She was trying to follow their talk. They had spoken of Peter McCue. It was still a logical question, she had only asked who he was, and Skeeter had turned and looked at Jim wild-eyed as if to say, "My God, don't your wife know nothin'?" Jim had laughed and explained that Peter McCue was the fastest quarter horse of all time and he added with pride that he was Pilot's granddaddy, but the rest of the evening when Skeeter looked at her it had been with a wary eye.

And polite! They were all too damn polite. The way they had of saying "Ma'am" to her was always disconcerting.

She had always been afraid of storms. She knew she had never really seen one until she came out here. The blinding flashes of lightning, the deafening crash of thunder overhead always panicked her. When she was alone she always pulled the covers over her head to shut out as much as she could.

That she would be alone at times had never entered her head. Jim had seemed to take it for granted — "You won't be spooked," he had said. Judy had shaken her head and she had given no intimation of how she felt when he rode off that morning driving a mount of horses before him. There was one that carried his bed. He had kissed her good-by at the water corral. "Only two weeks," he had said. She had stood at the gate of the water corral and watched him go. She had watched until he was but a speck in the distance, until he was out of sight.

When he had gone the country itself had changed. The great sweeps that stretched away as far as the eye could see became only empty spaces. She was conscious of its emptiness, her loneliness, the loneliness of it all. The flaming sunset she had seen that night had only depressed her more.

She had marked each day on the calendar. It was after midnight the seventh night when she heard him coming in. She had thrilled at the sound of the long-drawn cowboy yell, his way of letting her know who it was when he rode in at night. The roundup was camped at Bog Springs. It was only twenty miles. He must be back in camp at daybreak since he was on wrangle that morning. She knew he had ridden forty miles that night for only a couple of hours and she had forgotten her loneliness, she had forgotten everything until he rode away.

That was the way it always was. She always forgot everything until he rode away, then it all came surging back. All she ever did was wait. "The Johnson boy had laid out on the range three days an' nights with a broken leg before they had finally found him." What if Jim was hurt! What if she couldn't find him! Why was she always so helpless? Why was she always afraid of things, always afraid of herself? Jim was as much a part of the country as the hills themselves. Why didn't she belong?

The letter she had started that morning! With an effort she rose from the chair. Every fiber in her tired body ached as she walked to the kitchen table. Through the windows the first gray streaks of dawn were showing in the East. She forgot the dim lamp that still burned. She remembered each word she had written yet she read it again to herself.

Dearest, I know how you despise a coward, a quitter. Well, that's just what I am and I want you to know the truth. It isn't that I don't love you, it's just that I don't belong . . .

She had written it only that morning. Now why was everything changed? Or was it? Did anything change after all? The low, distant rumble of thunder brought her to with a start. There was the cow, the fool chickens, the horses to feed. She had forgotten them all last night. She had even forgotten Pilot after the run he had made. Jim was breathing easier now. She would have to hurry with the chores. She wanted to be beside him when he finally opened his eyes.

The rumble of thunder grew louder as she hurried outside the house. Steer Mountain was blotted out entirely. The storm was approaching fast. Let it come! She knew she would hide under the bedclothes again when she was alone, yet she almost welcomed it now. She would hang the nosebag on Pilot too, though she hoped she would never ride him again.

And she knew she would wait again through long, lonely nights, wait for Jim to come in. Yet somehow she felt strangely elated. Maybe she did belong.

NO BRACELETS

ONE of the outlaws was said to be riding a blaze-faced sorrel horse. He was a tall redheaded guy. It was thought he had held the horses while the other two robbed the train. He wasn't seen during the hold-up. As a matter of fact, the first report of the robbery didn't mention him at all. It said two men had done the job. They were cowpunchers of medium height, and both of them were masked.

It was the second report of the holdup that came into the sheriff's office two days later that carried the description of the tall redheaded rider and the blaze-faced horse he rode. A rancher on Coon Creek had seen the three outlaws together. They were heading south into Arizona. The report said, too, that the three men would no doubt split up on their way south and pass themselves off as cowhands.

It was just a happen-so that old Jap was in the sheriff's office when the second report came in. Jap seldom went to Globe. By doing his trading at the Indian Post he saved a twenty-mile ride. The Old Man's place was fifty miles from town. It was thirty to the Post. There was no road to Jap's little ranch. When the Old Man wanted a load of chuck, he forked a horse and packed it in on mules.

Old Jap just got back from town when the man rode into his camp. At any other time the Old Man would have welcomed the stranger with open arms. Jap was a friendly old cuss. But the sight of the blaze-faced sorrel horse and the tall redheaded rider was almost too much for him. In the first flurry of his excitement, the Old Man upset the coffeepot and kicked over a pot of frijoles.

Jack Blake was the name, the tall rider said. Old Jap, who had got control of himself, asked the stranger to get down. As the rider swung down from the big horse, Jap didn't miss a trick.

Blake carried a .30-30 carbine. It was the usual type of saddle gun commonly carried by cowboys on the range. Before Blake pulled the saddle off the big horse, he removed the gun from the scabbard and leaned it against a tree.

He carried no other weapon that Jap could see. It was just as the report had said. He had probably thrown his six-shooter away — or cached it with his share of the loot when the three outlaws had split up.

The big rider was quiet and cool. He was mighty sure of himself. But why didn't he ride a bay or brown? Some horse of a solid color. The big sorrel was too easy to spot. The man was a fool to ride a horse like that when he was on the dodge.

Jap had never seen the brand on the big horse. It didn't belong in the state. It looked like a northern brand to Old Jap, still he wasn't quite certain of that.

The big sorrel nuzzled the tall man as he stood by the horse's head, but when Jap happened to walk a little too close, the big sorrel flattened his ears. The big sorrel was a one-man horse. The horse was an outlaw, too.

Blake helped Old Jap prepare the evening meal. After supper they sat outside the cabin and smoked. To all appearances the tall rider was just a stray cowboy drifting through the country. He hoped to catch on with the H's, he said, he had heard they needed a peeler. He offered to take the edge off a bronc or two for Old Jap if he could stay and rest up for a few days.

It was with this understanding that the two men went to bed. It was hot in the little cabin, the room was stuffy at best. Blake casually said he would make his bed outside if it was all the same to Jap.

It was during the night that Old Jap hatched his plan. Next morning when he went out to wrangle the horses, he rode to Jim Bonehead's camp. Jim was an Apache Indian who was building some fence for Old Jap. The Old Man hurriedly scribbled a note for Jim to take to the trading post. The agent would phone it in.

The note said that the outlaw on the blaze-faced horse was at Jap's camp. He figgered to rest a few days. It would be better if the sheriff's office sent one man. Jap suggested Smoky Carver. If a posse came, some fool was apt to lose his head an' someone was sure to be killed. The big outlaw was quiet and cool as they come. Smoky never got excited much, Smoky would use his head.

And the Old Man's plan worked out all right. Smoky came next day. Jap and Blake were down in the horse corral when Smoky rode into camp. Blake was not ten feet from his rifle when Smoky rode in, yet he made no move for his gun. To all appearances the deputy was just some cowboy acquaintance of Jap's who had dropped in for a little chat.

Smoky greeted Old Jap and nodded to Blake before he swung down from his horse. It was all done in a casual way. But the instant the deputy's feet hit the ground, his pistol was out.

"Put 'em up, Mr. Outlaw," said Smoky. "You're wanted for robbin' a train."

"What the hell!" said the tall cowpuncher. "I can prove —"

"Never mind the talk," cut in Smoky, "just save yore alibi. You'll be needin' it, I figger, when we get

into town. Jap, be good enough to frisk the guy while I cover him. Nothin' on him, eh? Well, dump the shells from that thirty-thirty of his, an' catch me a fresh horse."

It had all worked out as Old Jap had planned, yet he wasn't proud of himself. To think of the tall rider

behind prison bars wasn't a pleasant thought. Just before they rode away, Jap turned to Blake and spoke.

"I'm sorry about all this," he said.

"Cut it," the tall puncher replied. "You only did
what you thought was right. Let's go," he said, nodding to Smoky.

For the first few miles they traveled the narrow
trail with Blake up in the lead where the deputy could
watch his man. But it was hard for Smoky's pony to
keep up, the way Blake's big horse was gaited. It was
Smoky who suggested that he ride in front, and that
Blake bring up the rear.

"An' don't run for it," said Smoky, "or I'll let the
daylight through you."

Neither man mentioned the holdup although they
spoke of other things. They chatted casually as they
rode along of conditions on the range. In this way the
two men traveled the trail from Old Jap's place down
to the trading post. Smoky, the deputy, in the lead, his
prisoner at his heels.

It was sundown when they reached the post. The
train was almost due that would take them into town.
The deputy and Blake were smoking in the horse corral when Smoky produced the handcuffs.

"They're not necessary," said Blake. "I'm perfectly willing to go to town with you and get this thing
cleared up. It's a wonder some granger didn't shoot me
off my horse, the way they had me posted. I'll admit
I rode a day with the outlaws. They were just cowpunchers to me when I first met up with them. When
they didn't act just right, I cut from them. I figgered

they'd pulled something, but I didn't know the train was robbed until you throwed down on me."

"Save it for the judge," said Smoky. "I ain't interested much. Come on, let's put the bracelets on. I hear the Passenger."

The tall puncher had spoken quietly, now he stooped as if to scratch a bite that was just below his knee. In a split-second he had whipped a six-shooter from a scabbard that was hidden inside his boot.

As Smoky faced the pistol, the deputy thought fast. What a fool he'd been! But why had the outlaw waited? He could have shot him off his horse at any time as they rode down the trail. Mebbe the tall guy had told the truth — ? Smoky was trying to figure it out when the puncher spoke again.

"Now you stand hitched, an' hear me out. Do you think if I was in on that holdup that I'd follow you all the way down here with a six-shooter in my boot? I'd have given you the pistol at the Old Man's place if you hadn't been so doggone fast. Now I'm perfectly willing to go to town with you an' clear myself — but I won't wear any bracelets."

Smoky drew a deep breath. "I reckon you win," he said. "An' do me a favor, please," said Smoky, as the puncher gave him the gun. "For cat's sake, don't mention that pistol trick you pulled on me or they'll laugh me out of town."

WOLF CALL

WE didn't expect to find anyone, least of all a woman. She stood in the half-light of the open door as Dogie an' me rode up.

I didn't say nothing so Dogie explained as how my pony had lost a shoe an' gone tender behind.

"We were hopin' to pick up an ole shoe," says Dogie. "We thought the cabin was empty. We're from the Bar F Bar."

She said they had only been there a month. She was sizing us up in the half-light. Her hair was red. She said we'd find some shoes down by the corral. She stood in the open door as Dogie an' me rode down.

"She's good lookin'," says Dogie, once we was out of earshot.

"She's young," I says.

"A hell of a place to bring a woman," says Dogie.

"She's young," I says.

I went through the pile of ole shoes until I found a number two. The light wasn't very good. Dogie found a rasp an' hammer in the shoe box. He couldn't find any nails. I shaped the shoe to the pony's foot. I could tell by the feel it fit all right but he was pretty tender. While Dogie was trying to straighten out some ole nails we saw a light go on in the house. Then she came out with a lantern.

"She's comin'," says Dogie.

I didn't say nothing. I was watching the woman. She held the lantern while I tacked on the shoe.

"That helps," says Dogie.

The pony was gentle but Dogie stood at his head. It took longer than common. The pony kept flinching.

"He's tender," says Dogie.

The pony was plated when she asked us to supper, I didn't say nothing. A coyote barked as we walked to the house. He was way back on the rim. I wanted to stay. I wanted to go in the room where she lived.

Dogie says we was a long way from camp an' we'd have to be drifting. I knew she felt better then. I felt better too.

She stood in the door with the lantern while Dogie an' me forked our ponies an' rode up the narrow trail. Dogie says it was a hell of a place to bring a woman. I didn't say nothing. Riding away from a light always made me feel lonesome. I could see the light in the cabin below us when Dogie an' me topped out. It looked lonesome too.

A nester had built the place. He had a woman an' some kids. The kids had always scuttled for the house or bushed like quail when one of us rode by. The woman had always closed the door.

Others had come and gone since then, starved out. They all starved out. They all tried to cultivate the little patch of brush an' rocks. They always had a worn-out team, a few poor cows. Their sharp-faced flat-breasted women had always closed the door when one of us rode by. Now she lived there.

He wasn't a nester like I thought. I knew he was her husband when he rode into our camp a month later at Soda Canyon. He was a cowboy. He was all man too. I watched him swing down from his horse.

Joe Martin, he said, was the name. We knew he was working on the Indian horses on that end of the reservation. Everybody stole from the Indians. It wasn't our affair. He said he had brought a little bunch of mares in from the north. I watched him as he talked. He smiled a lot. He was a tall, black-headed

guy with narrow hips. Her hair was red. He wouldn't stay an' eat. It was sundown when he left.

"It must be all of twenty miles," he says. "She's waitin' for me there."

I saw her once at headquarters when I went into the ranch for chuck. She had come to see Ole Ben. The Ole Man had carried her down a whole packload of fruit an' mason jars. She told Ole Ben she had put up fifty quarts of pears alone. The Ole Man called her girl. To him she talked as if she'd known him all her life. She was friendly to me too. She spoke about the night we stopped an' shod the horse. I couldn't talk. But it was nice to have her in the room. I stayed until she left for home.

They hadn't been married long, not quite a year. Ole Ben said her ole man owned an outfit in Montana. A good sized spread, it was. For a spell she had gone to school back East. Joe had been breaking horses at the ranch when she came home from school. Joe an' her ole man couldn't hit it off. Ole Ben said the girl had laughed an' said he guessed it right when Ben said he bet her ole man was a redhead too. She an' Joe had come to Arizona to try it on their own. They had drove a bunch of horses down.

After the day she came to the ranch I always stopped an' spoke when I was riding over there. She always asked me in. Yet I knew she always felt relieved when I wouldn't come inside. The only time I ever went inside the house was with Ole Ben. We had been hunting horses over on the river. It was sundown when we stopped.

We stayed an' eat. The place was snug. There was

curtains on the windows an' some flowers that was wet. She chatted with Ole Ben. I couldn't talk. I watched her light the lamp an' set the spread. Her body was young. Yet somehow she seemed old until he came.

At the first click of his pony's feet on the rocks she turned to us an' smiled. He was way back on the rim. She was at the door an' gone when he started down the narrow trail an' gave that long-drawn cowboy yell that resembles the wolf call.

The Ole Man looked at me an' smiled. We didn't speak till they came in.

"We've got company, Joe," she says.

He shook hands with Ole Ben an' me. He was bigger than I thought. Yet somehow he made me think of a cat when he walked outside to wash. Joe an' the woman chatted with Ole Ben until the meal was done. I couldn't talk. But it was nice to set an' watch her face. The smile was never gone from the time that he rode in. Finally Ole Ben slid back his chair.

"It's all of fifteen miles," he says, "I aint so young no more."

They stood outside the door as we rode up the narrow trail. When we topped out we both looked back. The place looked friendly now.

"She's happy," Ole Ben says.

I'd gone to the ranch again that day with a string of mules for some horseshoes an' some chuck. Ole Ben had just stirred up a bait for me when we saw the woman coming. The pony was weaving as he walked. I didn't think he'd make the house. Her face was white an' drawn.

"It's Joe," she says in a hollow voice. "He didn't

come in last night." I pulled the saddle off an' turned the pony loose when the Ole Man helped her down. The Ole Man tried to help her into the house but she wanted to walk alone.

I caught up three fresh horses in the corral an' threw the saddles on. Then I run back an' turned the pack mules loose. We might be gone for a spell. The Ole Man was giving her coffee when I came in the house.

"You've got to find him," she says to me. Her voice was high an' shrill. "My brother was killed that way. I know Joe's down out there some place alone with his horse on top of him."

"It's all right," I says. "We'll find him."

"It's all right," Ben says.

"I waited all night for the sound of his pony's feet an' his wolf call back on the rim. All I ever do is wait. I've rode every place an' called his name. You've got to find him, I say."

"It's all right," I says, "we'll find him. The horses is ready."

"It's all right," Ben says.

She seemed to feel better once we were mounted an' moving. She didn't know which way he had rode. I knew we'd have to cut for sign. We rode ten miles, I guess. I figgered on getting the outfit, twelve men was better than two. Then I spotted him.

She picked him up almost as soon as I did. He was heading down a long ridge with a bunch of wild ones he'd caught. He was heading for home.

She didn't speak. She sat on her pony an' watched

him. She was crying now for the first time. But she looked young again. I knew she wanted to go on alone. It was the Ole Man who spoke.

"It's tough," he says, "always waiting like you do."

She nodded her head an' smiled. She was looking down the long ridge. She was watching Joe when she spoke.

"It is tough," she says, "but somehow it's worth it when I see him riding in."

THE RING

HE had two wound stripes on his sleeve. I pegged him for a cowpuncher from his gait but the ring he wore was the first thing I noticed when he walked into the tent. I never wore a ring in my life, never wanted one before but I wanted this one.

It was after the Armistice at Camp Bowie, Texas. Yes, that was the first World War — the war to end all wars and make the world safe for the "Democrats." We had an open poker game going in our tent. It ran day an' night, off an' on, as there were only a few casuals going through the mill and we didn't stand any formations. A few of the lucky ones had managed to get discharged but most of us were still there four months after it was all over. We had it "via the latrine" that we were being held to help discharge the 36th Division when they got back from France. Lord only knew when that would be! In the meantime we played poker.

It was the usual Army game: dealer's choice, stud or draw, nothing wild, table stakes an' no limit. The game was full-handed this night. A couple of regulars, White an' Hoffman, who got in late were waiting for seats. A couple of casuals we didn't know were sitting in an' there were the usual ones who never played but

drifted in to watch awhile, then drifted out again.

This tall, black-headed guy who wore the ring stood just behind a casual who sat next to me. The tall guy didn't speak but watching him I knew he wanted in. This casual had no business in the game. Nothing was said, of course, but he seemed to be the only one in the tent who didn't know it. The cards were running good to him but twice he'd bet into a one-card draw an' been lucky enough to get away with it.

It finally came. The casual opened, drew two cards. I asked for one an' filled a little outside straight. He bet right into it. When I tapped him for all he had in front of him he called. He had three kings. It cleaned him.

When the tall guy made no move to take his seat I figured he was broke too but when I peeled off ten an' pointed to the ring he shook his head. When I doubled the ante he didn't speak, just shook his head again. But he stood an' watched until the game broke up around four A.M. an' we went out to eat.

It was drizzling rain when we filed out the tent. The only light that showed was in the Lone Star restaurant just across from camp. The tall guy headed down the company street the other way. You couldn't miss his walk. I wondered how long since he'd forked a horse. He turned an' walked on back when I said, "How about it, cowboy, come an' eat."

He was a cowpuncher all right, from the Panhandle. He was broke too. He just got into camp that day, he hadn't seen a payday in six months.

"That lamb that bet into your one-card draw," he said, "you wonder how he made it back from France alive. He had good cards tonight, some men will never learn."

He asked about the brush in Arizona, said he'd always worked in the open country. I said the brush wasn't so bad once a man got used to it.

"Wonder how it will feel to sit a horse again," he says. "Christ! I've walked ten thousand miles. It seems that many years since I've been gone."

We both had steak an' eggs. "The ring," I said, "I don't know why I wanted it, never wore one in my life."

"Lots of folks has wanted it," he says, "an' I've been broke." He didn't take it off but held it up where I could see.

The ring was made of gold an' stained by gas, so simple in design one wondered why it caught an' held your eye. "The inscription in the center seems to be Chinese."

"It is Chinese." He caught the question in my eye. "I took it off a Prussian officer." He didn't speak again until he'd pushed his plate away.

"It was a daylight raid, we went over after prisoners. They didn't put down a trial barrage an' we got caught in ours. The Sergeant had a Very pistol an' finally got it stopped. Then Jerry put one down that didn't miss an' we had boarcat hell.

"I don't know how many of us got over. Not over six or eight, I'd say. Three of us got back. The whole thing was hazy to me even then. Only certain things stand out. But it was this Prussian gent who killed Sarge an' got me through the left arm with a Luger gun. It's funny how little things stand out, his little waxed mustache, the little glass doodad in his eye, the way his lips were twisted in a snarl. An' even at the time it made me think of Joe, an ole ranch dog we had. Joe always curled his lip that way when he winded something that he couldn't see.

"When I let this hombre have it in the belly with a forty-five, he folded up. I let him have it twice, the second time for luck. An' then I saw the ring an' did a foolish thing. I reached down an' took it from him an' put it on my hand.

"I don't know whether that was when they got me through the leg or whether I got it going back. I didn't make it all the way. I got back through the wire, then my lights went out an' someone packed me in that night."

I was looking at the ring. He didn't take it off but held it close again.

"Lots of folks has tried to buy it from me like you did tonight an' I've been broke. Captain Spence, the doc who fixed me up, wanted to buy it too. He figured this Prussian gent had picked it up in China during the Boxer Rebellion."

I looked at the little inscription again. "Know what it means?"

"Yea, we had it translated. It means 'Thou shalt not kill.' "

OLD HAND

IT was Button's last night with the outfit. The spring roundup was over. He had turned in his string of company horses and caught up Blue Dog, his own mount. He and Blue Dog would start down the long trail again next morning. From his perch on the top rail of the corral he watched the old pony picking alfalfa down in the little horse trap just below the ranch house. The pony was fat as a seal. Little ole Blue Dog! He didn't look like the tired little horse that had carried Button into the Four Bar ranch that night just two months before. Honest ole Blue Dog. They had come a long way together.

It was almost three years since they had left the little farm in East Texas an' headed West for the big adventure. Button was fourteen then. He had run away to be a cowboy. It wasn't that they didn't treat him right at home. That was what made it so hard to leave. Yet somehow he had to go.

He had tried to explain it in the little note he left his mother on the kitchen table. Later she had written that she an' Dad both understood. Dad had been a cowboy too. But it hadn't been as simple as he thought. He hadn't made good yet. He couldn't hold a steady job. He was always the first one of the roundup crew to be laid off an' here he was most seventeen. He had begun to feel real old. No, it hadn't been as simple as he thought.

It was six months after he left home before he landed anything. His first job was wrangling horses at the L.F.D.'s in New Mexico. He had held that wrangling job until the work was through. From there he had rode the chuck line clear across the state, riding from ranch to ranch. He was welcome at every place he stopped. But at each ranch he was always told the same old thing — the outfit was full handed. If he had only come a few days earlier they might have put him on.

Button didn't realize until a long time later that the old hands made the talk to spare the feelings of a boy. Most of them had started out that way themselves. For except wrangling horses and acting as chore boy at the ranch, there was no work a boy or tenderfoot could do.

There were countless times when he missed the ranch he was heading for that Button laid out alone at night. At these lonely camps the pony had all the best of it. Blue Dog always grazed close at hand when he pulled the saddle off. Button's only gesture was to take up a notch in his belt. He soon learned that a drifting cowboy was much akin to the wolf. They both ate when they could. When he missed a meal the cowboy simply tightened his belt and rode.

On summer nights it wasn't so bad to curl up in his saddle blankets and lay blinking up at the stars. But as the nights began to grow cold he was always up and walking long before the morning star appeared, walking to keep warm.

It was when he lay out alone blinking up at the stars that home was most on his mind. He planned to go back for a visit when he was a regular hand. Yet the idea of going back to stay never once entered his head. Already the country was in his blood. He couldn't put it into words but in the great open flats and barren hills he had found something he'd always wanted.

Down on the Arizona line he caught on as chore boy at fifteen dollars a month. Button stayed a year. He didn't punch any cows, yet there was seldom a day slipped by but what he'd get a chance to try out a bucking horse. It was a straight horse outfit. The company ran no cattle. At first the peelers picked him easy mounts. But there are no short cuts to the game. All riders learn to ride a bucking horse by countless falls. When Button finally quit an' headed Blue Dog further west to try his wings again the boy could ride anything.

The work was different in Arizona too. There were always things to learn. A chuck wagon was sel-

dom used. Everything was packed. In Arizona Button
learned to throw a diamond hitch and to shoe a mount
of ponies. At times he wrangled horses through a work.
Often he rode as a cowhand. But always when the work
was through it meant the long ride down the chuck
line. It had seemed so simple when he started out. At
times he wondered if he would ever ketch on steady an'
be a regular hand.

Yes, there was more to punching cows than being
able to sit a bucking horse. It wasn't all roping either.
No man was a real cowhand until he knew what a critter was thinking of before the critter knew. Learning
to read brands and earmarks at a flash and to tell at a
glance when one was tampered with wasn't so easy
either. He had learned more at the Four Bars in the last
two months than ever before in his life. The Old Man
was a real cowman, so was Joe Morton, the foreman.
Joe knew every animal on the range as well as Button
knew his own mount of horses.

Joe had been mighty good to him too and never
once had the Old Man bawled him out after he'd pulled
a batter. The Old Man was easy to be around in spite
of his cold gray eyes. And the Four Bars was about the
prettiest spread he had ever seen in his life. Never at
any place he had ever worked had he rode such a good
mount of horses.

From his perch on the top rail of the corral his
eyes swept the Four Bar range. Night had already fall-
en. A lone coyote barked from the shadows of Horse
Mesa. He saw the light go on in the Old Man's room at
the end of the long ranch house.

He heard Joe Norton call Pete Jones. He watched
Pete detach himself from the group of punchers by the
saddle rack. Well, for once, at least, he hadn't been the
first to get his time. Pete was a good hand too. He
watched the other hands file in and out. Button had quit
his perch. He was almost to the saddle rack when he
heard his own name called.

The Old Man was seated at his desk. Joe was
squatted on his heels. It wasn't until the Old Man spoke
that things began to spin.

"You'll camp with Joe this summer, you'll ride the
same mount of horses. If there's anything you want in
town you can go in with the boys tomorrow, now that
you're on steady."

Button couldn't trust himself to speak. He could
only nod his head. He could only blink at Joe and nod
his head when Joe punched him in the ribs. It was all
he could do to reach the door, the room was spinning
too. It was almost like it was some times from the back
of a bucking horse.

Down in the little horse trap with Button's arms
around his neck Blue Dog heard it all. Of course, he
understood. Hadn't Button always told him everything
since they had been together? But it was nothing to cry
about. Why should Button sob? He was a regular cowhand now, he had a steady job.

THE GOAT

You've seen him in the movies lots of times. For there aint nobody doin' Western stuff that can sit a horse like him. He don't play a guitar and he don't sing. Fact is he don't do any parlor tricks. But any time he rides a bronk or ropes a steer you can bet your life there aint some cowboy doublin' for him. They've changed his name since he became a movie star.

But Si Smith was the way he signed it when he drew his sixty at the ranch. We called him Dogie Si an' Si is what he uses when he writes to one of us. For Dogie Si is always writin' us to come an' see his spread. He's off the women, so he says. But he's got a ranch all stocked with white-faced cows an' lots of fat horses for us to ride. An' Dogie Si says he'll get me a job in the movies any time I come. But ever since they took this picture at the ranch an' made me do that fall, somehow I'm not so keen for all this movie stuff.

It was because of this picture at the ranch that Dogie lost his girl an' got this movie job. An' even now when I see his name in big electric lights it's hard to realize that he's a star. For in this picture at the ranch they made him out a goat. An' Dogie wasn't even goin' when this movie outfit sent for him. For Dogie says no one could make a goat of him the second time. But the letter this movie outfit wrote him sounded straight

enough to us. An' along with it they sent a check. But at that I didn't think Dogie ever would have gone if he hadn't thought he'd get a chance to whip this Ham who queered him with his girl.

Katy was her name. She worked in "The Little Gem," a little quick and greasy joint just below the bridge. Katy wasn't no Mary Pickford for looks but she certainly had her own way around this eatin' joint. Me an' Dogie Si was together the night we stumbled into the place. The joint was full of hard-rock miners eatin' a bait before they went on graveyard shift. It seems a cowpuncher don't stand very high in that lay-out. For when I hung a spur on a table leg she bawled me out somethin' awful. Some Bohunk miner laughed. But when I asked him is there anything he'd like to say, he don't say nothin'. With that she opened up on me again.

Me an' Dogie finally slid into a couple of seats down near the end of the counter, but she don't pay us any mind until the mob clears out. She aint bad lookin' at that. I'm wonderin' what makes her wrists so red when she asks us what we'll have. She smiles at Dogie when he orders hot cakes. But when I says "The same," she gives me a look that makes me feel like crawlin' out of the place on all fours. She's pleasant enough to Dogie Si an' every time he says "Yes, ma'm," or "No, Ma'm," she fills his butter plate. My cakes is pretty dry, but I don't say nothin'.

Dogie Si was never much of a talker so by way of conversation he orders another stack of cakes. The game's a-gettin' good between them two. I might as

well be in camp alone for all the attention I'm gettin',
so when Dogie ordered his third stack I eased out in
the street.

It's funny what a woman can do to a man. Dogie
Si is a different person when I seen him again. He
wouldn't even take a drink.

"Katy don't like it," he says, "an' she won't stand
for no rough stuff. She's awful refined," says Dogie.
"She told me so herself an' she's got ideas. She's writin'
movie scenarios all the time."

I asked Dogie is she sellin' 'em but he don't know.
He never thought of that.

She even got Dogie to thinkin' about the movies.
One evenin' we're ridin' into camp alone an' Dogie up
an' tells me he thinks he's wastin' his time.

"Fightin' bronks for sixty a month aint much for
a man to be doin' that's got talents."

I figger mebbe he's right at that but it gives me an
awful shock just the same, comin' from Dogie. For
Dogie Si aint never done nothin' in his whole life 'cept
break horses an' punch cows.

"Katy thinks I'd photograph good, too," says
Dogie.

I aint so sure of that but I don't say nothin'.

When the outfit hit town Dogie Si spent all his
time a-hangin' around that eatin' joint. He kept away
from me an' Slim as if we was some kind of a disease.
The second day we met him comin' up the street. He
was dolled up so we didn't know him till he spoke. His
suit was bran-new. She'd even got a collar on him an'
some yeller shoes with buttons on the sides. Dogie

didn't look any too comfortable in the layout but he wouldn't take a drink. That night again we met 'em goin' to a show. I give 'em wagon room, but Slim don't know this gal. Slim thought he'd have a little fun. He stopped poor Dogie Si an' says he wants his suit an' asks why don't he pay the debts he owes. Poor Dogie grinned an' stood there sort of helpless like. The outfit laughed. Then Katy opened up.

It was the first movie outfit I'd ever seen. They drove into the ranch one night as if they owned the place. There's trucks and most two dozen cars, I guess. "Location," "local color," an' such don't mean nothin' to any of us. But they aint a bad outfit at that. Except the one they called the leadin' man. It seems that everything I says to him shore gets him on the prod. He got awful sore when I asked him is Tom Mix along an' when I says I like the way Mix sits a horse he acts as if he thinks I'm spoofin' him.

The leadin' woman's sort of pleasant like an' she could ride. She aint half as finicky as the leadin' man. One day I asked her where she learned to ride. She says her old man owns an outfit further north. It seems she don't think any more of this leadin' man than I do from the way she talks.

"He aint no cowpuncher," she says, "he's just a Ham."

They took pictures of most everything around the place. They even got old Sour Dough, the cook, a-washin' up the pots an' pans. They spent one whole morning takin' pictures of the ranch house. They took

a dozen of the Ham a walkin' in the door an' comin' out
again. In one he's wearin' Eastern clothes. An' then
they took some of him gittin' on his horse an' gittin' off
again. They took one of the girl a-standin' in the door.
An' then the Ham rides up with all his pretties on.
She's awful glad to see him from the way she acts. They
did it over twice. An' then they took one of her standin' in the door cryin'. They made her do it half a dozen
times. They finally took one of me an' Slim a-drivin' a
bunch of horses out of the corral. An' then they took a
dozen different ones of where the Ham's a-chasin' us.
In one they made me do a fall. I don't think much of
the idea when the director tells me about it, but he says
there's ten bucks in it so I take a chance.

We finally picked out a place where there aint
many rocks an' the cameraman set his outfit up. It
sounds simple enough the way the director explained it.

The Ham's to chase me an' Slim down in front of the camera. When the Ham shoots I fall.

"Let's do it right the first time," he says, "an' we'll only take it once."

We jogged up the wash about a hundred yards an' got behind some brush. I aint takin' any chances on gettin' shot so I examined the Ham's gun to make sure he's shootin' blanks. We get all set. The director waved his hand. Then we come bustin' out. The Ham was just behind. I tried to hold my pony in but he's hard-mouthed, we hadn't gone a dozen yards till he was simply flyin'.

It was an hour later when I come to. I'm thinkin' the gun was loaded after all. But they all said it was where I hit a rock.

They took everybody in the outfit at one time or another. But they used Dogie Si more than anybody else. They even let Dogie Si wear the leadin' man's clothes. They was just about the same size an' when Dogie got off a ways with that outfit on you'd swear he was the Ham. For Dogie aint bad lookin' at that. I didn't see the pictures they took down in the river. I aint able to ride yet but Slim said they shore was fine.

"The leadin' woman's game," he says. "The water was swift an' cold but she put her horse in without battin' an eye. Out in the middle she pulled him under. They flounder a minute. Then she turns loose an' drifts on down the stream. Dogie Si was wearin' the leadin' man's clothes. He hit the water from the other side. The current's pretty swift. She's a-needin' help, I'm thinkin', when Dogie pulled her up beside him on his

horse. They made 'em do it twice. The only time they
used the Ham was when they took a close-up of him
sittin' on his horse a-holdin' the leadin' woman in his
arms."

It was Dogie Si that rode the bronk too. They
picked out one we called the Apache Kid. He was a
spotted-lookin' houn'. But man! how he did wipe things
up. An' Dogie never made a better ride in his whole
life. My back's so lame I can't hardly get around but I
managed to get up on the corral fence so I could see
the fun. They finally got the Apache Kid blindfolded.
A puncher chewed his ear while they eased the saddle
on. Then I nearly fell off the corral fence. For up steps
this leadin' man dolled in all his pretty clothes. But he
don't ride the Kid. They only take some close-ups of
him just as if he's gettin' on. Then Dogie Si gets into
the leadin' man's clothes again. The cameraman moves
his outfit way back in the clear. Dogie swings up an'
caught his stirrups. The puncher jerked the blind an'
then the fun began.

My back still bothers me at times but except for
Dogie Si we've most forgot that movie stuff. Until one
day the boss come out from town, he says the picture's
on in town that night.

The whole outfit set together, exceptin' Dogie Si.
Him an' Katy had some seats way down in front. Old
Sour Dough can't see very well from where we're sittin' but he was afraid to move any further down for
fear Katy would charge him. An' Slim told me he was
actually uncomfortable jest bein' under the same roof

with that girl of Dogie Si's. We got there plenty early but by the time the show began the house was packed.

The picture opened up away back East. New York, I think it was. The Ham's a-wearin' evenin' clothes an' he's talkin' to a girl we've never seen before. It seems she's double-crossin' him but he don't know it. For she don't care nothin' for the Ham, only for his money. I'm actually feelin' sorry for the Ham the way he's gettin' double-crossed. But when he finds it out he gets all through with girls an' comes to Arizona.

He gets a job a-punchin' cows. He caught on mighty quick, I'd say. For he aint there no time at all before he's ridin' bronks an' showin' the old punchers how to rope stock. Then we all laughed for there's old Sour Dough, the cook, a-foolin' with the pots an' pans. It seems this leadin' woman owns the ranch. She's awful sweet on this new hand. But he don't pay her any mind. She's havin' an awful tough time too. For there's a mortgage on the ranch an' the neighbors is a-stealin' her blind. It shows two hombres drivin' a bunch of horses out of the corral at night. An' I'll be blowed if it aint Slim and me. They've made a horse thief outta both of us. An' then the Ham gets sorry for the girl an' starts to chasin' us. The crowd all started clappin' when we made that run an' when I did that fall I thought the kids down front would go hog-wild.

An' then it shows the Ham a-ridin' off. The girl's a-standin' in the door a-cryin'. She thinks he's gone for good. She gets her horse an' goes to take a ride. That's where the river stuff comes in. Her horse won't swim. But she don't care. She's just about to drown an' then

the Ham comes bustin' in just in the nick of time an'
pulls her up beside him on his horse.

It seems he never meant to go away. He's only
been to town to fix the mortgage up. For this Ham is
grass-bellied with spot cash. It shows a close-up of him
settin' on his horse. He puts his arm around her. Then
the thing fades out.

Dogie Si was alone when we met him. He's still
a-wearin' them yeller shoes but he aint got no collar
on an' it don't take a man with more than half an eye
to see that he's been drinkin'.

"What's the trouble?" says Slim.

"Trouble?" says Dogie Si. "There won't be anything but trouble when I find that leadin' man. That
double-crossin' Ham. He's made me out a liar.

"You know I wouldn't lie to a girl," says Dogie,
"at least not about anything as simple as ridin' a bronk
or swimmin' the river. Katy don't think much of cowpunchers nohow. She keeps tellin' me all along she'd
never marry a cowpuncher. If I was a movie actor
things might be different. Naturally when we take this
movie at the ranch I tell her about some of the things
I've done. She thinks it's pretty fine. She's awful interested in the movies an' we don't talk about much else.
I'm goin' awful strong — till they show this film."
Dogie rolled a cigarette.

" 'The leadin' man is wonderful,' she says. But I keep
tellin' her to wait till I do that stuff of mine. They
finally rope the Apache Kid an' put the blindfold on.
'Now watch!' says I, a-gettin' set. 'Here's where I do
that ride.' I can't believe my eyes at first. Then Katy

looks at me an' sort of sniffs. 'Looks like the leadin'
man to me,' she says. 'There must be some mistake,'
says I. 'Just wait till they show the river stuff.'

"It shows the girl a-driftin' down the stream. The
Ham rides in an' swings her up beside him on his horse.
An' then a close-up of him with his arm around the girl.
The thing fades out but I'm not in this film at all. I'm
sittin' there wonderin' whether I'm afoot or horseback
when Katy brings me to.

" 'You lyin' pup,' she says, 'you're just like all the
rest.'

"I looked around — but Katy's gone. She's left me
talkin' to myself."

TIN HORN

No one cared much when Dopey left the Wine Glass outfit unless it was Bill Wilson. An' Bill saw red for quite a while each time he thought about them fancy boots of his that Dopey took. Slim Higgins said that Dopey was welcome to that "45" of his that disappeared when Dopey left. For Slim says if Dopey handled it like he did a rope there was always a chance that he might shoot himself.

Dopey came to the outfit when Old Buck owned the spread. The outfit found him sittin' on the ranch-house porch one day when they got in. At first glance the punchers took him for a peeler who was driftin' through. For some of those birds are long on pretty clothes an' go in strong for fancy rigs. An' Dopey was dressed as if he'd just left Hollywood. His clothes all showed some wear but his Stetson was a 7X. An' the scarf he wore around his neck was knotted in the latest movie style. His boots was scuffed an' showed that they'd been used a heap more on the ground than on a horse. But them fancy colored butterflies stitched in the tops would make any cowdog bat his eye. But Dopey soon proved what he was — a tin horn an' a tenderfoot.

Right off the bat he told a big one how he come to be afoot. Of how his horse jerked from him when he got down to get a drink. He even described his outfit in detail an' told what brands was on his big bay horse. An' the funny part about it was that yarn went down with all the boys. Two Wine Glass punchers hunted for his horse next day. They took Dopey's trail right at the ranch an' back-tracked it to the spring where he had got a drink. There was lots of fresh horse sign at the spring but none of them was shod. This had the punchers up a stump for Dopey had said his big bay horse was plated all around. But the boys cut sign an' then finally found Dopey's track where he had walked into the spring afoot. An' from there they trailed it to the main highway where he had evidently quit some car, for that was where his track played out.

The chances are good if they had got a holt of Dopey then that he never would have lied no more. But they had cooled off some when they got in that night an' all they did was cuss him out. For when they faced him with the facts Dopey admitted without shame that he had never had a horse.

At first he spoke of different outfits where he'd worked an' of the horses he had rode. But Dopey soon found the cow game can't be bluffed an' he was smart enough to cut that out. An' he finally admitted that the Wine Glass outfit was the first real cow spread he had ever seen. An' that all his ideas of a ranch an' cowboys come from Western stories in the magazines an' from Western movies he had seen. An' he had worked as an extra in several Westerns while he was in Hollywood. At least, that's what he said an' it accounted for his pretty clothes.

He said he came from some place back in Illinois an' that story sounded good until he changed it later to New York. For somehow Dopey couldn't tell the truth. At that, his stories never hurt anyone but him an' the boys got so they all enjoyed his tales. An' lots of evenins 'round the fire some puncher would sing out, "Come on now, Dopey, tell us all a lie."

Most anybody would have run this tin horn off. But Old Buck always fed every stray dog that ever showed up at the ranch an' he let Dopey stay an' sweat — work for his chuck, I mean. Dopey did chores around the ranch an' rode the pasture fence. Old Buck give him Happy Jack to ride when he was out messin' around an' them two was a pair, for Happy Jack was almost as sorry a horse as Dopey was a man.

Happy Jack was a good lookin' pony. But he was the kind of a horse no real cowboy would have in his mount. He was just another one of them good lookin' horses that wasn't worth a dime. But to watch Dopey ride in on Happy Jack, a man not knowin' the pair would have figured Dopey for a real cowhand an' Happy Jack for his top horse. For Dopey was easy to look at on a horse or on the ground an' even after his pretty clothes wore out a man would look twice at him.

Things rocked along through the summer. Dopey stayed an' sweat. He won enough money playin' cards to keep himself in tobacco. The boys figgered he was crooked an' watched him like a hawk. But he was too smooth with the pasteboards to ever get caught cheatin'. But any pot of any size just naturally went to Dopey. He could do card tricks by the hour no one could see through. An' the things he could do with a pair of dice — well, he could make the ivories talk.

The outfit was short handed when the roundup started in the fall so Buck put Dopey on the payroll an' let him wrangle horses. An' Dopey took as much pride in that lousy job as if he owned the layout. An' for a tenderfoot he done pretty well for he didn't lose many horses.

Buck cut him four ponies to ride along with Happy Jack. A couple was pretty fair ponies but Dopey couldn't tell the difference between a good horse an' a sorry one an' Happy Jack was Dopey's favorite.

Sometimes at night he'd tell a big one, what he done that day while he was herdin' horses an' the boys would string him on. He'd tell of how he branded some big calf or mebbe got his rope on some wild horse. But always some little thing went wrong like breakin' the hondoo in his loop, for Dopey never led no wild ones in. The boys all knowed he never could get close enough to anything to even get a throw when he was ridin' Happy Jack. For it was always Happy Jack he rode in all of his wild stories.

As soon as the steers was shipped that fall the outfit all went into town. Slim Higgins had a girl who
was slingin' hash at a quick an' dirty joint just below
the bridge an' Slim was buildin' quite a stack to her.
Slim took her to the movies that first night an' stayed
sober as a judge. Dopey was settin' in a stud game further down the street an' he never showed up at the
restaurant. But when he blowed in for a meal next day
an' Slim's gal got one flash at him the outfit knowed
Slim's time was beat. Dopey had evidently made a lick
in the stud game. For his new boots alone would have
cost a month's wrangler's wages.

Slim laughed about it when Dopey took her to a
show that night. Slim said he didn't care, talked real
sensible at first an' says he didn't want no truck with
any gal who couldn't tell a tin horn from a real cowhand. But after Slim got sixteen drinks he changed his
tune an' started lookin' for Dopey with a gun. But after
his twentieth drink Slim got down an' the outfit drug
him off to bed so there wasn't any killin'.

But next mornin' Slim was still on the prod when
he woke up, the likker was pretty bad. An' when he
found Dopey in the restaurant with his gal, Slim give
him his choice of comin' outside an' takin' a lickin' or
takin' it right there. An' Dopey bellered like a calf an'
begged Slim not to hit him. Now we all supposed a
woman wouldn't have no truck with a man who
wouldn't fight. But this gal turned on Slim an' scratched
his face an' cussed him out an' finally made him leave
the place, an' she hung right on to Dopey.

Old Buck had paid Dopey off an' let him go along

with the other new hands who worked in the roundup crew before they come to town. An' the outfit figgered they'd seen the last of Dopey when they got back to the ranch. But it wasn't a week before he showed up at the ranch again an' went right back to sweatin', an' Old Buck let him have his mount of horses back an' let him ride with the outfit.

Horses was Old Buck's weakness. The Wine Glass range was full of old cow horses that had served their time an' Old Buck had pensioned an' set free. An' for all his lyin' an' sneakin' tricks Dopey was good to a horse. That was the only reason the outfit could ever figger that Old Buck let him stay. For Dopey never did make a cowhand no matter how hard he tried. If they didn't watch him like a hawk he was sure to mess up a drive. An' usually when he tried to head a steer back in the bunch he wound up by runnin' him off. For Dopey never did learn the nature of a critter or understand their ways. So Old Buck put him to doin' chores again an' ridin' pasture fence. When the roundup was goin' on Buck let him wrangle horses. Any man with any pride would have quit an' gone away. Anyone could ride Dopey for the tin horn wouldn't fight. But Dopey was perfectly satisfied just to be around a horse. Most punchers will talk to a cow horse when they're alone with him. But he would visit with Happy Jack no matter who was around.

"Best cow horse in the world," he'd say. An' Happy Jack would nod his head. "Come on now, pardner, an' shake hands." An' Happy Jack would shake. But Dopey couldn't have caught a cow on him if his life hung on the deal.

Dopey stayed two years. An' the chances are good that he would be at the Wine Glass outfit yet if Old Buck still had the spread.

But with the drop in prices an' the drought Old Buck went broke an' turned the outfit over to the bank. Old Buck never said a word but the boys all figgered it was pretty tough. The outfit had been his for forty years. He'd built it up from nothin' when the range was free. But Old Buck wasn't a business man. An' he rode down the trail one evenin' just at dark without once lookin' back.

Miller bought the outfit from the bank. An' he hadn't been in charge a week before he run Dopey off an' told him never to show his face at the ranch again. None of the hands blamed Miller but at that the boys all hated to see Dopey leave for they all enjoyed his lyin'. Everyone knowed he was helpless as a hand but they figgered he was harmless.

Dopey was flat broke when Miller told him to hit the trail. So Slim an' Bill Wilson staked him to enough to get back out to Hollywood an' when Dopey left he stole that pretty pair of boots from Bill an' took Slim's gun by way of showin' his gratitude.

The next move that Miller made, the hands all quit. For the first work that Miller done when he took over the spread was to round up all the condemned horses he could find on the Wine Glass range an' peddle them to the Apache Indians.

Old cow horses that had served their time an' Old Buck had pensioned an' set free. Honest old ponies that had more than earned what little grass they eat if they

had lived a hundred years. It was just as well for Miller
that Old Buck didn't know.

Before he quit, Slim Higgins gave Miller twenty
dollars for two old ponies he had rode when he first
went to work for Buck. Slim had no place to run them.
But Slim figgered a "45" slug between their eyes was
easier on them than to carry some fat Indian all day,
then stand half starved all night in front of an Apache
tepee.

Two years went by. The old Wine Glass outfit
was scattered. Some of the boys were at the Circles an'
OG-Rail. Old Buck was drivin' team down at the
Coolidge Dam. Slim an' Bill were at the Cherries.

Dopey had been in Hollywood two years an' he
was comin' back. For the Western movies had just
about played out an' extra work was scarce. But Dopey
still dressed in the latest movie-cowboy style. An' the
first tourist he flagged out on the road was going
through Arizona. The tourist was glad to buy Dopey's

meals. An' I imagine after he got back East the tourist often spoke of the real cowboy that he'd picked up who was tryin' to get back to his range. For Dopey told him he was just a waddie from the sticks who was having his first look at Hollywood an' Dopey laughed about the way them city slickers had picked him clean. Dopey cussed the lousy movies.

It was long in the evening of the second day when they came in sight of the Wine Glass range. Dopey was full of stories. An' the tourist was so impressed he stopped his car when Dopey pointed out a hill to him where a bronk had bucked him off. But most of the stories Dopey told were of himself an' Happy Jack, wild horse races on the mesa an' of big steers they had caught. "Best cow horse I ever had my saddle on." The tourist was impressed.

Dopey had figgered on going further on where he wasn't known so well. For he hadn't forgotten them boots of Bill's or the six-shooter he took from Slim. But when he saw dust comin' from the shipping pens it was

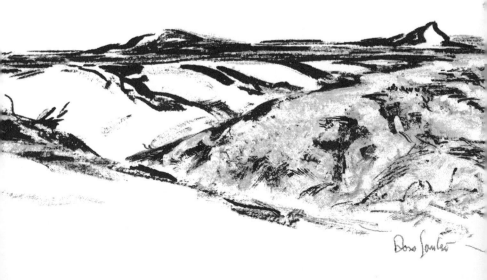

more than he could stand. For Dopey had helped ship cattle from those very chutes. An' he was willing to even risk the lickin' he knew he'd get if he met Bill or Slim for a look inside them.

"Here's where I get out," he said, an' he shook the tourist's hand an' thanked him for what he'd done. "Guess it feels pretty good to be getting back again," the tourist said. "Things never looked so good before," says Dopey as he waved his hand, "for those ole hills is home."

But Dopey saw no cowboys that he knew as he climbed up on the fence. For there were only two Apache cowboys there an' an old cowhand Dopey had never seen inspecting a bunch of horses. But the ponies were old friends of his an' Dopey knew them all. Yep! there was little ole Sunshine, a pet of Buck's, an' Scout, a horse that was in Slim's mount, an' Poky, one of Bill's. The ponies were bunched in a corner of the shipping pens an' Dopey could only see his ears but he knew at once it was Happy Jack. Old Happy, his top horse. Dopey was just ready to crawl down in the pen for a visit with him when the inspector spoke to him.

"This is the lousiest job I've ever done, inspectin' these ole ponies. I don't wonder Miller sent his two gut-eaters along with them considerin' where they're goin'. Of course, it's none of my business for the horses belong to him. But he's shippin' these ole ponies to be killed for dog feed over on the coast for a measly three dollars a head. I've needed three dollars pretty bad at times but there's some things I wouldn't do. Goin' into Globe? I'll be glad to carry you."

Dopey didn't trust himself to speak so he just shook his head.

As soon as the inspector left, Miller's two Apache cowboys tied the gate an' rode on up the wash to a tepee that they knew. They had nothing to do but visit with their friends till the horses were loaded next morning.

The tulapia was good that night an' the Apaches sat up late. It wasn't until an hour before shipping time next morning that they showed up at the pens. An' there was considerable panic between the two right then for the horses were all gone. Someone must have opened the gate. But by cutting sign an' ridin' their horses half to death the Indians rounded up all of them in time to ship — except Happy Jack. It was queer how Happy would pull out by himself an' quit the other horses.

The Cherries were shipping cattle some thirty miles below. Slim Higgins was on day herd. Slim thought he must be seein' things when he looked up the river. For the rider looked like Dopey an' the horse was Happy Jack. But as they kept on getting closer Slim knew that he was right. A dozen things passed through Slim's mind. He'd waited long for this.

There was that money he'd loaned, his six-shooter an' Bill's boots. Well, anyway, when he got through with him this time no girl would look at Dopey.

But Dopey told the truth this time. Slim knew he wasn't lyin'. An' Slim forgot the lickin' he had promised him. For Slim Higgins loved a horse an' the story Dopey told squared everything with Slim.

"Ya mean to say ya stole the saddle too?" Slim asked.

Dopey nodded yes.

"Well, keep to the river till ya get below the high cutbanks," said Slim, "an' no one is apt to see ya."

"Guess who I seen today?" says Slim as he an' Bill Wilson were taking the remuda out that night. "You'd never guess — Dopey!"

"That sorry son of a bitch," says Bill. "I spose ya worked him over?"

"No sir," says Slim, "I let him go for I felt sorry for him."

"I think he's about the sorriest hombre I ever run acrost," says Bill.

Slim shook his head. "I'll admit he's pretty sorry but he ain't half as sorry to my mind as a man who'd sell an old cow horse for three bucks an' let 'em make dog feed of him."

THE RUMMY KID GOES HOME

HOME, to an Arizona cowpuncher, usually means any horse he happens to have his saddle on. But to the Rummy Kid it always meant Chicago. An' Chicago to the Rummy Kid meant tall buildings by the lake.

Sentinel Butte always made Rummy think of the old water tower. An' when Rummy was out on the mesa with the ponies he had only to half close his eyes an' the mesa became a lake an' the rimrock was a row of buildings — tall buildings by the lake with the boats for Michigan City an' Milwaukee an' the little boats that ran to Lincoln Park.

Once when Rummy an' Johnny McHale had been swimming out to the breakwater from the foot of Ohio Street one of those little boats had almost run Johnny down. Johnny McHale — say now, there was a regular guy. No kids had ever picked on Rummy when Johnny was around. It was Johnny's folks who had taken Rummy in to live with them when Rummy's father died. They ran the little corner saloon an' grocery store on St. Clair Street where the teamsters all hung out.

Rummy could see the teamsters, too, sitting on those high stools at the bar drinking scoops of beer.

71

Blackie Shannon always said it was the biggest five-cent beer in town. Bigger than anything that even Hinky Dink put out at the Working Man's Exchange. Blackie Shannon ought to know, for didn't he drive a brewery team? An' there was Big McShane — say now, there was a real guy too. He drove the four big blacks for the Calumet Baking Company. No teamsters ever got fresh with him, no matter how drunk they were. Once Big Mac had beat another teamster near to death for saying that Frank Chance was a better first baseman than Jiggs Donahue.

Rummy was a White Sox fan himself an' he didn't blame Big Mac. But somehow it always made him sick inside when he thought of how the teamster looked when they pulled Mac off of him. But Mac had shore been good to him. Most every Sunday when the Sox were home, Big Mac took him with him to the old Sox Park. An' Mac was never too busy to stop the four big blacks. Even in traffic too, while Rummy climbed up beside him on the driver's seat. An' Big Mac always let him hold the lines whenever he filled his pipe. An' just to set up on the seat an' hold those lines had always sent a thrill through Rummy.

Rummy didn't remember his father much. But Big Mac had known him well. It always made Rummy feel good inside when Big Mac spoke of him.

"Bye," he'd say, "I never seen yer auld man's beat at drivin' team. Yer auld man knowed a horse."

Rummy had always intended to be a teamster too, till the circus came along.

He an' Johnny McHale had sneaked inside that

day with a lot of other kids. He hadn't intended to run away till he saw the circus horses. Rummy could never understand that part of it or why he felt that way. But whenever he looked at a good horse something pinched him in the throat. One look at Sultan, High Noon an' Silver King had been too much for him. But it wouldn't have been so hard to leave if Johnny McHale had only come. Rummy had cried himself to sleep in the horse car lots of nights at the thought of leaving Johnny. Johnny McHale — say now, no one had ever picked on him when Johnny was around.

Slim Higgins found the Rummy Kid in Globe. The circus had gone broke. An' like a lost dog Rummy had been hanging around the Lodge Saloon not knowing where to go.

Slim was breaking horses over on Cherry Creek. He was just a hand himself. But Slim had a weakness for stray dogs an' he took Rummy out to the ranch with him. Slim had only been fourteen himself when he ran away from home.

Rummy stayed at the ranch with Slim till the fall work began. Then Ribs, the foreman, put him on an' let him wrangle horses. An' the Rummy Kid was quick to learn. He had a feel for horses.

As soon as the punchers were mounted for the day the remuda was turned over to Rummy. If the outfit wanted a change that day he brought the ponies into camp at noon. But the kid was by himself all day with his band of saddle horses. An' for the first time since he ran away Rummy was really happy.

Rummy had been with the outfit most a month

when he saw his first wild horse. He was hunting a lost
saddle horse that day when he jumped the wild bunch
out. Rummy often ran the wild ones after that an' it
always gave him a thrill. But he never forgot the race
that day, or his first look at the Buckskin Stud.

He was riding a big stout horse that Slim had
staked him to. As the Kid rode out of the cedars he
came suddenly on the bunch. It was just a happen-so,
he had the wind on them for the wild ones were all
grazing — all except the Buckskin Stud, an' he was
standing guard.

The Buckskin whistled at sight of the Kid an' the
wild bunch left with a jar, all except the Buckskin leader, who trotted toward the Kid. Something pinched
Rummy in the throat. For neither Sultan or Old Silver
King could match this horse he saw. As the Buckskin
came on closer Rummy took in all his points, from the
broad forehead an' deep chest to the way he was cou-

pled up. It all happened in an instant. Then the Buckskin leader whirled an' went flying across the mesa with
the Kid in hot pursuit. There was four miles across that
open flat with the sting of the wind in his face. The
thunder of those flying hoofs, the big black that fell an'
broke his neck. As they came down off the rocky side
of the mesa, Rummy could have touched a big bay ma-
verick with his hand. The wild ones were all about him
and the Kid was unafraid. His eyes were on the flying
Buckskin out in front.

The wild bunch ranged from the Big Valley to the
rim over toward High Point. On days when his horses
were quiet Rummy often slipped away to ride down
the long limestone ridge that overlooked the Valley.

Near the end of the ridge the Kid always slid from
his pony an' dropped his bridle reins. Then pulling off
his old felt hat he would crawl to the big flat rock that
gave a view of the whole Valley. For just to watch the
wild bunch grazing always gave him a thrill. An' the
sight of that Buckskin stallion always pinched him in
the throat. Sometimes he watched them for hours before he slipped away. But often his pony would nicker
an' frighten the bunch below. Then Rummy would
wave his old felt hat an' yell as the wild ones raced
down the Valley.

Rummy had been in Arizona two years when he
began to talk about going home. That was in the winter. He planned to be in Chicago by the Fourth of
July, he said, he planned to stay a month. He hadn't
been to town since Christmas an' he would have six
months' wages coming.

"So yer a-goin' to take in the bright lights, Kid?" Old Ribs would say. "Wish I was goin' with ya, must be lots of wimmin an' booze,."

"Chicago's a regular town all right." An' the Kid would shake his head. But Rummy never spoke to anyone of what he really intended to do.

He an' Johnny McHale would swim every day at the foot of Ohio Street. An' he'd ride a lot with Big Mac. An' he'd buy the tickets on Sundays when they went out to the White Sox Park. Wouldn't the kids all stare at his big hat an' high-heeled boots? An' they hadn't better make any wise cracks about them either when Johnny McHale was around. He planned to take Johnny a pair of spurs an' he'd take Big Mac a quirt.

The outfit all rode into town the week before the Fourth. There were nine cowboys in the bunch. As soon as they put their horses in the corral they headed for the first saloon an' lined up at the bar. Ribs bought the first round. Slim the next. An' then came Rummy's turn. Rummy got that down all right but by the time the last man bought a drink, things had begun to whirl. He could hear the punchers talking but it sounded a long way off.

"So yer headin' for the bright lights, Kid," boomed Ribs. "Let's have another round."

Slim found the Kid at midnight asleep in the corral. The Kid was holding a pair of silver-mounted spurs an' a braided rawhide quirt. When Slim went through his pockets he found four silver dollars. But the Kid's six months' wages were gone.

Slim put the Kid to bed an' next morning except

for a bad taste in his mouth the Rummy Kid was feeling fine. He couldn't remember much about the night before, or where his money had gone. He vaguely remembered playing the roulette wheel. He thought he had won. But the spinning wheel had made him sick an' he vaguely remembered moving over to the crap table where things didn't whirl so much.

"Well, don't let it bother ya," said Slim. "You're not the first cowpuncher that ever missed his trip. It's happened to all of us, I reckon. I've planned to go home at Christmas time for fifteen years an' I aint made it yet."

So Rummy spent the Fourth in Globe. It wasn't what he'd planned. But the rodeo in the ball park lasted for a week an' Rummy enjoyed it all. For Slim Higgins rode Old 41, an old outlaw from Bloody Basin with a rep — the whole outfit was down on the ride an' Slim spurred the old outlaw from shoulders to rump till Old 41's head came up. Say now — if he could ever make a hand like Slim! An' Slim had entered Rummy in the team-tying with him an' they had won third money.

It seemed to Rummy that everyone in the grandstand could hear his heart a-thumping as he waited for the steer to leave the chute. He hoped he wouldn't let Slim down. Rummy was to rope the old steer by the horns. Then Slim would heel him an' stretch him out while Rummy tied the two hind legs.

It seemed an age to Rummy before they ever turned the old steer out. But once he heard Slim yell, "Let 'im go," the Rummy Kid was cool. An' Rummy made a clean throw an' caught the steer by the horns. But Slim had to use two loops before he picked up both hind feet or they would have won first money.

Then Ribs, the foreman, tied three calves for an average of twenty-one seconds. Say now — there wasn't an outfit there that had made a better showing. It made a guy feel good to belong to a spread like that. An' he had done his share, for didn't he ketch his steer with just one loop?

It was only when he looked at the silver-mounted spurs for Johnny an' the braided rawhide quirt for Big Mac that the Rummy Kid felt sorry.

Six years slipped by. Rummy was a full-fledged cowhand now. He didn't wrangle horses. An' Rummy never spoke about going home again. For the boys still teased him some about that Fourth in Globe.

"When ya goin' home, Rummy?" some puncher would sing out. Then Rummy would always grin an' try to laugh it off. But deep down inside it hurt. For in his war bag Rummy still carried the silver-mounted spurs an' the braided rawhide quirt. Several times he had the money saved. But like the real cowboy Rummy was, it always slipped away.

It was seldom that Rummy was out on the mesa now. His job was with the cattle. But whenever he rode that way Sentinel Butte always made him think of the old water tower an' the mesa became a lake. An' the rimrock was always a row of buildings to him — tall buildings by the lake. The wild bunch still ranged from the Big Valley to the rimrock over toward High Point. But the Kid never rode down the long limestone ridge an' crawled out to the big flat rock any more. For the Buckskin leader was dead.

Ribs sent the Kid to hunt a saddle horse the wrangler had lost that day. The horse was the 66 Bay. Rummy struck his track at the bronk corral. He was heading toward the cedars. As Rummy followed the track at a walk he knew that if he didn't overtake the horse he would come out on the mesa at the same old place where he had first seen the wild bunch. If the 66 Bay got in with them he was shore to have a race. But he was riding Black Diamond that day an' Blackie was his top horse. Well, anyway, if the wild bunch happened to be grazing near he had the wind on them.

As the Kid rode out of the cedars he forgot the 66 Bay. For the wild bunch were all grazing again. An' there was a Buckskin stud. At sight of the Kid he whistled an' the wild bunch left on high. Something pinched Rummy in the throat again as the leader trotted toward him.

As the Buckskin came on toward him, Rummy never moved. But as the Buckskin whirled an' raced away the Kid shook out his loop.

For a mile the race was even. Then Black Diamond began to gain. Rummy could feel the big black's heart a-pounding now up against his knee. The wild ones had scattered like a covey of quail as Black Diamond raced through the bunch. Rummy could easily have roped the 66 Bay. But the kid saw only one horse that day an' it was a Buckskin stud.

The Buckskin was taking the broken ground. Like a swallow he raced along. Black Diamond's breath was coming in a great sobbing sound and Rummy was cutting the blood from the big black now at every jump with the double of his rope. For the Buckskin was slipping away. Then with a crash the big black horse went down an' the Buckskin stud was gone.

It all happened in an instant. One of Rummy's spurs had hung. The big black horse rolled over him as he went crashing to the ground.

The Rummy Kid lay very still. He felt no pain. He wasn't even conscious of the fact that a dead horse lay on him. For Rummy was watching the little boats that ran to Lincoln Park. He could see the old water tower again. Sure, he'd take a ride with Big Mac. He an' Johnny McHale were swimming again at the foot of Ohio Street. "Look out, Johnny, for the boat" — that one had almost got him. The breakwater looked a long way off today. A fog was settling down. But he knew he'd make it all right with Johnny McHale along. Johnny McHale — say now . . .

The Rummy Kid had gone home.

LOWER TRAIL

W<small>E</small> never knew how it started. Some trifling thing, I suppose. But it grew until both cowpunchers were ready to shoot on sight.

Jim had come to Arizona from Texas. Charlie was from the North. The two punchers had been friendly enough when they came to work at the outfit.

They broke horses together that summer and worked in the same corral. When it came to making a hand, there was nothing to choose between them. Both boys were plenty salty and inclined to be highstrung. If either was jealous in any way, they never showed it.

They range-branded together that winter and slept in the same tepee. If there was any trouble between them then, we never heard of it. It wasn't until a long time after Jim quit riding for the Turtle's and went over to the Dart's that we noticed they didn't speak.

Things rocked along for a year that way. Charlie never mentioned Jim's name. Occasionally one of the punchers would drop some word in camp about something Jim had said, trifling things and said in fun, for they could see it bothered Charlie.

There's always some punchers who love a row and like to rib a fight. Some of the boys began to pack yarns into camp about things Jim had said: "Charlie couldn't ride in a wagon, Charlie would starve to death in camp if he had to ketch his own beef."

Meaning, of course, in plain language, that Charlie was not a good rider and he was no hand with a rope. Later, we found that they were doing the same at the Dart's, stampin' a load into Jim.

I liked both boys myself and it bothered me. Any man with half an eye could see where things were headin'. But when I spoke to Charlie, it didn't clear things up.

"First thing I know there's anything stickin' in Jim's craw, I meet up with him in town. I ain't seen Jim in some time. He don't speak to me. But if that's the way that hombre feels, it's quite all right with me."

I mentioned loose talk to Charlie, but I didn't get very far.

"You know I've never said a word against him in my life," he says. "You'd better make your talk to Jim."

Not long before the showdown came, Charlie and I were both in town and we run into Jim.

"Hello," says Jim to me, a-flashin' that grin of his I always liked so well. "How's everything at the Turtle's?"

Jim halfway looked at Charlie as if he would like to speak. But Charlie was staring straight ahead. He never looked at Jim. At that I could see Jim redden right through his coat of tan. After making some poor excuse about watering his horse, he walked on down the street.

That night as we rode back to camp, I tried to

patch things up again. Charlie wouldn't even talk when I spoke to him of Jim.

Our outfit was camped at Stray Horse. Charlie was shoeing a pony when old Miller rode into camp. Old Miller said he had come from the Dart's, said that he had seen Jim and Jim was packing a gun. Old Miller figgered Charlie ought to know just what was going on. It was common talk among the Dart cowhands that Jim intended to kill Charlie the first time they met up.

Naturally, we looked at Charlie while Miller was airin' his paunch. Charlie didn't say a word. As soon as he got his pony plated, he rode out to the herd.

As a usual thing, Charlie never packed a six-shooter, he carried it in his bed. But the morning after old Miller rode into camp, Charlie was wearing his gun.

There was no way to avoid a meeting. It would be settled that day. We were moving our herd south, and from what old Miller told us, the Dart's were coming our way. No matter what had caused it all, it meant but one thing now. The showdown had finally come. Either Jim or Charlie, or mebbe both of them, had seen his last sunrise.

We pushed the herd off the bed ground that morning long before daybreak. It must have been two that evening when we sighted the dust ahead. The Dart's were coming from the south, so we throwed our herd off to the left so the two herds wouldn't mix.

Charlie helped throw the cattle out. Then he rode up to the boss. If Charlie had been yellow, he wouldn't have made this move. He knew that certain hands were bound to say he was afraid of meeting Jim.

"Jim's comin' yonder," he says. "You know the talk he's made. I've got nothin' against him, so I'm takin' the lower trail." With that he wheeled his horse an' loped away as the Dart leaders came in sight.

The Dart foreman was riding up on point. We spot Skeet Johnson next. We figger Jim is back with the drags. The dust was pretty thick. As soon as their herd came alongside, Skeet rode over to us.

"Where's Charlie?" he says, a-lookin' around. When we told him about Charlie taking the lower trail, Skeet looked mighty queer.

"Jim took the lower trail himself," he says, "to keep from meeting Charlie!"

The Dart herd finally faded into the dust. We let our cattle graze. I don't know how long we waited. It seemed like an age to me.

"Looks like Jim's got Charlie," the foreman finally says. Two of us were fixing to take the lower trail and look for him, when Charlie rode up to the herd. Right then I hated Charlie, I'd thought a lot of Jim. But all of us gathered around when Charlie began to speak.

"I'm lopin' along the lower trail," he says, "a-wonderin' if I done right to put the showdown off, a-thinkin' about this thing, when I see a rider comin' — damned, if it aint Jim! He's lopin' too, until he ketches sight of me. Then he pulls his pony up and we ride toward each other at a walk, watchin' each other like hawks.

"Jim never used to pack a gun. But I see he's got one now. That aint like Jim. It don't seem right. Then it occurs to me, I'm packin' one myself. But it's him that's made the fightin' talk, so I wait for him to draw.

"A thousand things flit through my head as we

ride toward each other. Most of them triflin', too. One of the silver conchos on Jim's bridle has worked loose. I wonder if he knows it. What will he say before he starts to shoot? Mebbe he won't speak! The distance now, I'd say, is twenty yards. Why don't he pull his gun an' start the thing? It's him that's made the talk. I wonder if he still packs the branding iron I made for him when we was camped together. It can't be Jim I see!

"I'm lookin' at a man I've never known. His eyes are hard like flint. His face is like a mask. Now I know it means the end for both of us if he pulls his gun. We wasn't ten feet apart, then I hear him speak —

" 'Hello, Charlie,' I hear him say in a voice as cold as ice. 'Hello, Jim,' I says to him, still waitin' for him to draw. We were that close, I could have kicked his pony in the belly with my tap as we rode past each other.

"We've passed each other, mebbe fifteen feet, when I take a look around. Kind of a sidelong glance I take to see just what he's doin'. Damned, if Jim aint doin' the same — he's just lookin' around at me.

"I don't know why I did it. Things was still pretty tight. But the idea of us two a-tryin' to dodge each other, an' meetin' up this way struck me funny all at once. Damned if I didn't laugh.

"At that Jim wheeled his horse around an' flashed that old grin of his. It was the same old Jim I knew. Neither of us says a word, but Jim put out his paw. It aint till after we shake hands that either of us speak. We don't say much then.

" 'I think we're both damn fools,' says Jim. Then we shook hands again."

A COWPUNCHER'S LETTERS
FROM HOLLYWOOD

D EAR Slim,
    I'm in Hollywood. I left the ranch a week ago
an' if I ketch on in the movies, Arizona will be shy one
more good cowhand when the roundup starts next
Spring.

I'm livin' acrost the street from the Water Hole.
That's a place where the movie cowpunchers hang out
an' I've run acrost several punchers I've knowed in
Arizona who are workin' in the movies here. I've
picked up a few things from them but these movie
cowpunchers don't put out much information so most
everything I've found out about the town I've had to
pick up myself. I aint what you'd call city broke yet
but I know where all the studios are located. I've got a
map of the city so I go most every place in the Hoopie
now without much trouble but it bothered me some at
first.

You know I drove over in the Hoopie. I never had
no trouble comin' over but comin' into Los Angeles a
cop waved me down the first turn I made. I figgered
I'd pulled some kind of a batter but I didn't know what
until he asked me didn't they use no signals in Colorado?

"I don't know," I says, "I aint never been to Colorado." An' then he asked me what I'm doin' with a

Colorado license on my flivver. So I told him about the
trade I'd made with some hombre who came by the
ranch.

"Where ya from" says he, an' when I says "Globe,
Arizona," he says most of the trouble they have over
here is with folks that drives over from Globe.

"Well, I'm a cowpuncher," I says, "an' I don't live
in town."

"That's worse yet," he says. An' then he advises me to park the Hoopie some place an' take a cab or street car for any travelin' I do in town. He says there's plenty of parkin' places further on an' after sayin' he'd like to see the two horses I traded for this wreck I was drivin' he motioned me to go on. I guess he figgered I got stung in that trade but I didn't, even if the Hoopie wouldn't run at all. For one of them ponies was locoed an' I guess you know that little Quarter Circle gray? It was the other one an' if that hombre from Colorado is able to get a mile from camp without him givin' out under him it was more than I ever could.

After the cop turned me loose I headed the Hoopie right on down the street a lookin' for a parkin' place. But I never had no luck. There wasn't no chance to turn off the street for there was cars on both sides of me an' every corner was marked either "no right turn" or "no left turn" or "no parkin' here" so I kept right on down the street in the middle of the drive. I drove for an hour, I guess. I'd come to thinkin' I'd have to drive

right on through town without stoppin' but finally the traffic thinned out a bit an' when I saw a sign that says "parkin'" I herded the Hoopie in there. I was afraid to put out my arm for fear I'd get it knocked off but I made it in all right without gettin' the Hoopie cut in two.

I left my saddle an' the rest of my outfit in the Hoopie. But I took my suit-case an' walked back up the street until I found a hotel. I got me a room an' after cleanin' up some I et a big bait an' went out to take in the sights.

You know a man comin' from the country don't have no idea how many people there is until he comes to town. I milled around with the crowd until my feet got to hurtin' an' then I took in a show. It was when I come out of the show that I got mixed up for when I started back to the hotel, I never could find the place. I'd forgot the name of the hotel so I couldn't ask no-body. But I knowed it an' the theater an' the place where Hoopie was parked was all on the same street. So I walked until my feet was afire an' then I hired a cab. I told him to drive me around until I finally gave it up an' told him to take me to some hotel he knowed. He charged me twelve dollars for the ride an' I got me another room an' hit the hay.

It was just an accident that I finally found the place next day. I got me a cab first thing in the mornin' an' had him drive me around again an' then I tried the street cars for a while but there wasn't no place I seen that looked familiar. So I took another cab. These twelve dollar rides was cuttin' into my roll pretty heavy but walkin' was out of the question for I was wearin' a new pair of boots. An' my feet was still hurtin' from that walkin' I'd done the night before. So I kept a playin' first the cabs, then the street cars until along about three the next day. The feller that was drivin' the cab must have figgered I was crazy for I'd have him drive me up one street as far as it went and then take the next one back. Finally he asked me what was the trouble for he seen I was lookin' for something. I told him he couldn't help me none for I didn't know the name of the hotel. But I told him the whole yarn anyway. An' when I told him about the Hoopie an' the hotel an' the theater all bein' on the same street he says I must have a parkin' ticket for the Hoopie. An' shore enough I did. An' it didn't take him no time until he found the place.

The Hoopie was there all right an' a little further up the street was the hotel an' I had him drive me up the street until we found the theater too. They was all on the same street an' I'd had the direction right the night before so I couldn't figger out how I'd missed the hotel. But the feller who was drivin' the cab says I probably come out of the theater on another street from what I went in. It never occurred to me that there was more than one door to the place so I guess that's what I done. Well, live n' learn. That's what the Ole Man always told me at the ranch. That's what I'm doin' now. But if I ever get back to Arizona I'll never laugh at another tenderfoot who comes out to the ranch.

SHORTY

Dear Slim,

Well, I've finally caught on in the movies. I've only worked one day but I got twenty five dollars for that. They pay ten dollars for an extra, but when a man doubles like I done today they pay extra for that. But a man shore earns his money when he doubles. For I'm still so sore from that fall I took I feel like I'd been beat with a pole.

Yesterday I went out to the studio but I went to the wrong place. For I didn't know this outfit had two places. When I got into the office there was several people sittin' around an' the feller who was back of the fence never even looked up when I come in. I stood there like a horse for a minute an' I was beginnin' to feel like one too for nobody paid me no mind. Finally I knocked on the fence an' says "How-doo."

"What do you want?" he says, without lookin' up. An' when I told him I'd like to see the director he asks me which one. I didn't know they had more than one but I says I want to see the one who directs the western pictures. "Have you got an appointment?" he says. I told him I didn't but I'd like to see the director anyway. But he says, "You can't see a director without an appointment." So I went out of the place.

This mornin' I went out to their place in the country. They was makin' a picture out here. I didn't have no pass so I looked the lay-out over for a while an' finally I seen several people goin' back an' forth that didn't show no passes. So I throwed in with them. I was wearin' my boots an' big hat so I guess the gateman thought I was workin' there too for I got inside of the place without nobody stoppin' me.

I hunted up the foreman who was in charge of the stables an' I didn't have no trouble talkin' to him for he was an old cowpuncher. He says they only want men who can ride for this picture but I look like a cowpuncher an' talk like one an' if somebody don't show up that's near enough my size so I can wear his uniform he'll take a chance on me.

I stayed right at that hombre's heels for an hour. Finally he pointed out a little sorrel horse an' says I can ride him. He says I'm to be a cossack cavalryman. An' after lookin' in his little book he gives me a number an' points out the place where I'm to get my uniform. When I showed them the number they gave me the uniform without no trouble. But I couldn't find a place to put it on. Finally I asked a feller where I could change my clothes an' he says "anywhere." But there was people millin' all over the place an' lots of women too. I saw one hombre a changin' right out in the open but that was too much for me. I finally spotted a shed that was off a ways an' I laid my uniform down until I looked it over. The shed was open on two sides but I decided to take a chance but when I came back to get my uniform it was gone. Then the foreman rode up an' asked me why wasn't I in costume. An' I told him somebody had hi-graded my clothes. "Where's your horse?" he says. "He's right over there," I says, "unless somebody has stole him too." An' then the foreman says I aint at no cow ranch now an' after I've been around here a while I'll know better than to lay anything down on a movie lot if I ever expect to see it again. But he says if I can pick out my uniform he'll

pull it off the hombre that's wearin' it. But there was
three hundred men a wearin' uniforms just like mine so
I knowed that wasn't no use.

It was the first time I was ever inside of a movie
lot. So I looked the place over an' the whole thing was
mighty interesting to me. For there was most everything one could imagine that goes into the makin' of
pictures.

Old fashioned ox carts from Mexico, stage coaches
an' prairie schooners. A corral full of Mexican steers
along side of a pen full of camels. An' most every kind
of stock from an English thoroughbred on down to an
Indian cayuse. One end of the place looked like an old
fashioned cow town. It looked mighty good to me
until I found there was nothin' to the buildings but
false fronts. They must have had three hundred head of
horses. Of course the horses interested me more than
anything else. An' I was down in the stables lookin'
them over when I run into the foreman again. He asked
me if I wanted to do a stunt. I didn't know what he was
talkin' about but I says, "Yes." An' then he tells me the
feller who was to take the fall wouldn't go on with the
thing. After I looked the layout over I can't say I
blamed him none. For they dug a hole about four feet
deep right in the middle of the road. The hole was filled
with straw an' my stunt was to come down the road an'
hit that hole with my horse on the dead run.

The director didn't do much explainin'. I'm an
outlaw, he says. An' as I come down the road I'm to
shoot at some fellers that's chasin' me. There's cameras
stationed all along the road to ketch me as I go by. An'

I'm to time my shots an' shoot the last one just before we hit the hole.

I've took plenty of falls out on the range when there wasn't no straw to fall on. But I never got one like this before. For when we hit the hole the old horse turned plumb over an' lit on top of me. I never had nothin' hurt me as much in my whole life before. An' if I'd been killed it wouldn't have made no difference to them for they went right on with the picture.

For the bunch that was a chasin' me rides round the hole in the road an' instead of givin' me a hand when they gets off their horses they start proddin' me in the ribs with their six shooters an' me a needin' air so bad I can't even cuss. All this time the director's a yellin' orders at everybody at once. An' after they've prodded me in the ribs with their six shooters until they get tired of that he tells 'em to hand-cuff me an' put me on a horse. I never got my breath until the whole thing was over. Once I got enough air in me so I could talk I says plenty. But the director gave me twenty-five bucks an' he says the fall was a pip. The director tells me I can make a heap more money by doublin' than by just workin' extra. Twenty-five bucks aint bad for one day's work when you come to think it over. But if a man makes his livin' by doublin' I don't figger he's apt to live more than a week.

Watch for the "Rustler's Revenge." That's the name of the picture I'm in. Of course, I aint seen the picture yet so don't know how good the rest of it is. But there wasn't no fakin' about that fall of mine.

SHORTY

Dear Slim,

I've had some hard luck since I wrote you last. For somebody broke into my room while I was asleep an' stole my pants along with what money I had which was ninety four dollars. But he overlooked an old pair of levis that was hangin' on the wall so I put them on an' by hockin' the Hoopie with the landlady I raised enough money to eat. That same afternoon they called up from the studio an' asked would I do another stunt. They didn't say what it was but I says "Yes" for I needed the money. But if somebody hadn't stole my pants I wouldn't have took it for I was still so sore from that last fall I took, I could hardly walk. But this was the easiest twenty five bucks I ever earned for all I did was to ride a pitchin' horse.

They was ready to start shootin' when I got out to the lot an' it surprises me some when the director tells me I'm to ride a buckin' horse. For the leadin' man is standin' there too, dolled out in all his pretty clothes. I sposed, of course, they'd have him ride the bronk. For I'd seen this leadin' man ride in pictures lots of times an' from what I'd seen of his ridin' he was a he-wolf on a horse. But the stable foreman tells me this leadin' man couldn't ride in a covered wagon unless both ends was shut tight.

First thing they do is to drive an old gray horse into the corral. This old gray is gentle but he's roped an' jerked around for a while an' then a puncher goes down the line an' ears him down while they put on a hackamore an' the blind. Actin' all the time like he's a raw bronk. They ease on the saddle an' cinch the old

gray up so tight he can't hardly breathe so naturally he squirms around like a young horse would.

The director says this leadin' man is a stray cowboy huntin' for work an' they've caught this horse up to see can he ride. An' when the director gets through his talk the leadin' man eases into the saddle. He takes the hackamore rope in one hand, his hat in the other an' as he gets all set to meet the first jolt the director yells "cut." The leadin' man dismounts an' after the old gray is unsaddled an' led off they drive another gray horse into the corral.

There's no foolin' about this horse for he's shore enough kinky. As soon as he's ready I'm told to put on the leadin' man's clothes an' do just as he had done. The cameras is all moved back a ways an' when I gets all set they slip the blind an' turn the pony loose.

He wasn't a hard buckin' horse to ride for I could scratch him any place I pleased. I fanned him with my hat until he finally quit pitchin'. An' as soon as the director yells "cut" I got hold of an ear an' stepped off. He's unsaddled an' turned loose an' they bring in the gentle horse again. The leadin' man gets into his pretty clothes an' as soon as the old gray is saddled he rides him off a ways an' when the director gives the signal he heads the old gray straight for one of the cameras. He grabs holt of an ear an' steps off just like I done with the bronk. An' then he unsaddles the old gray an' turns him loose right in front of the camera. Evidently he's put up a whale of a ride for he's hired right now. The punchers all shakes his hand an' after they do most everything except kiss him the director yells "cut."

Ya know, this don't look right to me. Everybody thinkin' this leadin man is a he-wolf on a horse when he can't ride in a wagon an' I tells the stable foreman what I think. But he says that even if this Ham could ride a pitchin' horse they wouldn't let him for he might get hurt an' hold up the picture. An' they could always get plenty of waddies like myself to double for them things for if we get hurt they're not put out no way. That may be one way of lookin' at the thing. But just the same I wouldn't think this leadin' man could look a real cowboy in the eye.

Shorty

Dear Slim,

I've come near drowndin' since I wrote you last. For I got off so easy when I rode the buckin' horse I says "yes" when they called up from the studio an' asked would I do another stunt. The name of this pic-

ture is "The Orphant." I'm the Orphant's old man with
the long white whiskers who is washed down the canyon an' drowned.

The movie outfit built this canyon but it shore
looked natural for they had bushes an' things planted
all along the sides of the thing. I didn't think much of
this idea of bein' washed away but the director says I'm
only to be washed down about forty feet an' then the
canyon spreads out so's the water aint deep. He says a
man can't be drowned in only goin' that far so I decided to take a chance.

When the cameras was all ready they brings up an
ole horse an' buggy an' me an' the Orphant gets in. The
director says I'm to drive down to the edge of the water
an' leave the Orphant on the bank just as if I'm goin'
to find out if it's safe before I take the Orphant acrost.
There's only about a foot of water comin' down. But
there's two fellers who is hid from the cameras a shov-
elin' mud in the water so's nobody can tell how deep
the water is. Every little while they'd throw in a bush
or the limb of a tree an' the thing shore looked spooky
to me. The Orphant aint in no danger for I leave him
on the bank but when I drove about half way acrost
they turned eight feet of water loose on me. I took
plenty of air when I seen this water comin' an' it was
a good thing I did for I never got no more air until I
came out down below. For when that eight feet of
water hit us it washed me an' the ole horse an' buggy
all down the canyon together. I washed loose from the
buggy when the water hit us an' it was lucky for me
that I did. For the ole horse an' buggy rolled over an'

over together an' when the whole thing was over the
ole horse was occupyin' the seat where me an' the Orphant had been.

They gave me fifty dollars for the stunt. But I
wouldn't go through with the thing again for nothin'.
For if I'd had to go ten feet further I'm thinkin' I would
have been drownded.

SHORTY

Dear Slim,

I caught on as an extra yesterday with another
movie outfit that's a startin' a big western. An' if somebody don't steal my clothes in the meantime I'm supposed to work tomorrow. But you can't tell what's
goin' to happen from one day to the next out here.
When I got out to their place this mornin' it looked
like all Los Angeles was huntin' for work. I've never
seen such a crowd in my whole life before. There was
an ole man with long white whiskers, slick faced kids
an' ole ham actors, cowpunchers an' more pretty girls
than we got cows at home. I figgered my chances of
ketchin' on was mighty slim for I didn't know nobody
but I decided to stick around anyway an' see how the
thing was done.

We all stood there like a bunch of gentle cattle
until some hombre gets up on a box. But when he says
he wants ten men that's six feet tall an' weighs two hundred pounds the stampede was on. Me bein' a runt, that
let me out but I come near bein' tramped to death when
the rush started. For there must a been two hundred

men a tryin' to get to him. He finally cut out ten head he wanted an' the herd got sort of quiet again. But it still was mighty restless for every time he'd point out someone in the crowd there'd be a dozen charge him. He'd cut out forty, I guess, when finally he points at me an' says "you little fellow." I'm standin' between two fellers that's all of six feet tall an' they both charge him but he waves 'em back an' had me to come up. He had me turn around an' anyone would think he's lookin' for a spavin or a ringbone the way he looks me over. An' after doin' everything 'cept look in my mouth he cuts me through a gate.

After I'm out through this gate I'm run through the chute while another hombre looks us over again. He's explainin' all the time that they don't want nobody 'cept cowpunchers an' if a man don't know how to handle a horse they don't want him. There's plenty in the bunch that wouldn't know a cow from a steer yearlin' but they don't say nothin'. There's a feller up ahead of me that rooms at the same place I do. He's never been on the range in his life. But he gets by as a cowboy an' I'm glad he does. For he's a pretty decent feller even if he does write western scenarios an' make his livin' workin' extra in the movies.

This hombre who's lookin' us over asks everyone some questions an' then he puts their name an' address in a little book he has. They all got past without trouble. But when he comes to me he asks me what I'm doin' here for he says they only want real punchers. "I claim to be one of them animals," I says. "That's what they all say," says he. An' then he tells me to step over to one side. I figger mebbe it's because I'm wearin' a cap. For ever since they had that piece in the Los Angeles paper about a movie cowboy snatchin' a woman's purse I aint been none too proud of that big hat of mine. But just the same if this hombre can't tell a real cowpuncher when he sees one no matter what he's wearin' I aint a goin' to argue the thing with him. I figger I'm out of luck an' I aint really carin' much for this bein' herded 'round and its getting on my nerves. But this feller who writes the scenarios sees I'm in some kind of a jack pot an' when he finds out what the trouble is he says he'll vouch for me. When he tells this Ham that I'm an Arizona puncher who's never done nothin' 'cept break horses an' punch cows he says he'll take a chance on me.

This picture that I'm workin' in is just like all the rest I've seen. Today we chased the hero through the hills an' tomorrow he'll chase us. I spose we'll have the pretty girl who's captured by bandits an' after the hero shoots all his ammunition up, of course he'll rescue her. We'll have the usual amount of cuttin' an' shootin' the director thinks is necessary an' after the hero an' the pretty girl has clinched they'll call the picture done. Ya know, I'm gettin' a belly-full of this here movie stuff an' as soon as this picture's finished I'm goin' to roll my tail for home.

SHORTY

Dear Slim,

I doubled for the leadin' man today. The feller who was to do the stunt must have got cold feet. Anyway he didn't show up. I wouldn't have done the stunt either but my bank roll wasn't none too fat an' I knowed if I come back to the ranch broke I'd never hear the last of it. But I got fifty dollars for the stunt an' I got off without a scratch.

As usual the director didn't do much explainin'. After I gets into the leadin' man's clothes he says I'm bein' chased by bandits. They think they've got me penned up on a bluff. But I jump my horse off the bluff into a water hole an' get away.

The cameras is all ready an' the director is rarin' to go. But I wanted to see where I was to go off the bluff. I left the ole horse back a ways for I knowed if he seen the place I'd never get him off. It shore looked spooky when I looked over an' the bluff looked more'n twenty-five feet high to me. But the director says that's all it was. I asked him how much water is there in the hole. He says there's six feet of water so I decided to take a chance. But I did a heap of thinkin' on my way back to my horse. For if we come to the bluff slow an' the old pony tried to slide I knowed he'd turn plumb over an' if he did I knowed it would be all day with me. So I figgers it's safer to bring him up fast for in that way he'll shore have to jump.

I wasn't wearin' no spurs so I borrowed a heavy quirt. I'm supposed to be shootin' as we come up to the bluff an' I'm supposed to shoot my last shot at the fellers that's chasin' me just as we go over. But I don't obey orders here for once we start I shoot as fast as I can pull the trigger an' when the gun is empty I throw the thing an' use that quirt.

We come up to the bluff with me a pullin' the quirt off the ole pony's flank at every jump. It couldn't have worked better. For the pony never had no chance to check himself an' he jumped just as high as he could. When we hit the water he was right side up an' we went to the bottom too. Of course, the water checked the fall an' I never got no jar at all. But when we hit the bottom I could feel the ole pony's legs buckle. When we come to the top I swam on out. But the pore ole pony, he nearly drownded an' we had to drag him out. Ya know, I figger that's givin' a horse a dirty deal. For a man gets paid for the chances he takes an' it's up to him as to whether he takes it or leaves it but a horse aint got no say.

It wasn't until I come to thinkin' about the jump afterwards that I got scared. For just as the pony jumped an' while he was in the air he nickered an' you know that's somethin' a horse wont do unless he figgers he's in danger. For you mind the time the bull got Wicker Bill's horse penned up against the bluff an' how he nickered just before the bull got to him?

I got a letter yesterday from Wicker Bill. He says it's rainin' at the ranch an' everythin' is greenin' up back there an' there's lots of white-faced calves showin' up. He says the Ole Man aint let no one ride my string of horses yet for he figgers I'll be back as soon as I get a belly-full of Hollywood. He won't have long to wait, I guess. For if someone don't steal my clothes tonight I'll write you next time from the ranch. For I'm goin' home tomorrow.

SHORTY

THE ORCHARD

THE men were coming off shift when the man was murdered. It was shortly after midnight when they left the change room at the mine. They had walked down the track as far as Rollie Coleman's. Rollie's joint is just below the smelter. The killer appeared suddenly from behind a coke car.

The killer was masked. He wore a handkerchief tied over his face and he carried a .30-30 carbine, a short saddle gun commonly used by cowboys on the Arizona range. The men thought it was a holdup until Bell, a miner, called the man by name.

"Dick Raines!" he shouted. "For God's sake, Raines, don't shoot!" Bell was begging for his life when Dick Raines shot him down.

Dick Raines was a cowboy who was working in the mine. When Smoky Carver, a deputy, picked him up a few days later at the Three Deuces ranch he readily admitted the killing; Bell, he said, had been too friendly with his wife.

Little was known of Bell, the murdered man. The sheriff's office traced him back to Butte, Montana. He had no kin. The man had worked at the Buffalo mine a year. His affair with Dick Raines' wife was apparently known to everybody on the hill. It was intimated, too, that Bell hadn't been the only one. It was common talk along the street that the woman was not worth killing anybody over.

While a killing was not uncommon in the mining camp, the thing had been badly done. Why did Raines wear a mask? Why did he run away? It was nothing but coldblooded murder. He was guilty as hell, they said. If he had given Bell a break, or shot him down in broad daylight upon the street, he might have cleared himself. Hawkins, better known as Old Smoothie, was defending Raines. Well, he had better be smooth this time for the odds were ten to one that Raines would hang.

But when the trial was held a few months later it caused no more than passing interest. The miner, Bell, was dead; he had no friends. The jury was drawn from the range. Raines' wife was young, still in her early twenties. Men found her easy to look at on the stand. In a choking voice she sobbed her story to the court. She readily admitted her relationship with Bell; the man had forced himself upon her, so she said. Raines' wife was young. The miner, Bell, was dead.

Hawkins, Raines' lawyer, offered no defense. He only asked to let the cowboy tell his story to the court. Dick Raines was tall and strong. He was young, not much older than his wife. He didn't belong in the mine. He spoke in the slow, laconic drawl of his kind. The man belonged to the range.

Yes, he knew of Bell's visits to his house; the man had been his friend. They had worked on opposite shifts at the mine. He had no doubts, nor any reason to suspect, until his wife had come to him in tears that night and begged him to take her away. His wife had told him everything. It was then he had rushed from the house and killed the man. He didn't know why he had worn a mask, or why he had run away.

After the killing he rode back to their little ranch in the hills. He sat in the orchard there. The little orchard had been hers, she had planted the trees herself. The orchard had been her favorite spot, it was where he usually found her when he came in from the range. As he spoke of his wife and their little place in the hills the cowboy's eyes were misty. Apparently it was hard for him to speak, so deep was his emotion. It was there they had planned together, they had been so deeply in love.

They had lived on the little ranch three years, he had taken her there as a bride. He spoke of their happiness and their hopes. But times had been hard on the range. They didn't have many cattle. There was no other out but to go to town and get a job in the mine. Even after they went to town they had planned to go back; the little ranch was home. Now everything was shot to hell. They would never see it together again.

It was the smell of the peach blossoms that morning that finally drove him away from the place, it was more than he could bear. When he left the ranch he had wandered aimlessly. He didn't know where he had gone. Smoky, the deputy, had picked him up at the Three Deuces. He was glad that Smoky had come.

As the cowboy finished his story emotion ran high in the room. An old cowpuncher, who had killed his man, cried openly, unashamed. Raines' story made a tremendous impression upon everyone. So simple and honest, they said. The cowboy's wife rushed to his outstretched arms when the jury acquitted him.

There was something hauntingly familiar about

Raines' wife to hard-bitten Smoky, the deputy, as he
watched her in the courtroom. It might have been
Cripple Creek, Colorado, or again it could have been
Hovey's on the Frisco — some of the dance-hall girls
were young and as pretty as so many speckled pups,
and Smoky had been around. But it was the story of
the orchard he couldn't get out of his head. When the
cowboy told the story that day Smoky could smell the
blossoms again. He could picture the little ranch house,
the corrals and the orchard the girl had planted, where
she waited for her cowboy when he came riding in.
Back in the long ago there had been a peach orchard
where he played as a kid. The story haunted him.

It was a few weeks later that Smoky made a
twenty-mile ride out of his way just to see the little
place. It was sundown when the deputy sighted the
little ranch, and he could hardly believe his eyes. There
in the basin below him stood the ranch house and the
corrals as he had pictured them, but except for a few
scrub willows at the spring there was not a tree in
sight. The peach orchard was a myth.

For a moment he sat stunned. Well, what the hell;
he wasn't the only one who had been taken in by the
story of the orchard. Old Smoothie, the lawyer, had
put one over again. Smoky had ridden down to water
his horse when the woman appeared at the door.

As the woman appraised him her eyes grew
friendly, warm. . . . Raines had gone on a horse hunt,
he wouldn't be back for several days. Wouldn't the
deputy unsaddle, wouldn't he get down?

It was with mixed emotions that the deputy sat

his horse. "I reckon not," he said. "I just dropped by to take a look at the orchard."

As she spoke she laughed a mirthless laugh. "So you fell for the story, too? Don't you remember me, Smoky? I thought you knew me all the time — from the dance hall, in Cripple Creek. I remembered you."

The big deputy shook his head. "There was something familiar about your face. But it was the orchard I came to see."

She laughed again. "Old Smoothie put it over. Mebbe you know Dick, or mebbe you don't. When Smoothie hashed up the story Dick says, 'Why, there's no orchard there!' But old Smoothie worked on him so long Dick not only believed the story, he could smell the blossoms, too."

Smoky shifted in the saddle. "Well, you put on a pretty good act yourself."

She laughed again and it wasn't pleasant to hear. "That was Old Smoothie too. In the first place, there was no cause for Dick to kill the man. He wasn't the only one. I was goin' nuts in that little dump in town, just like I'm goin' crazy here. That was the reason we went to town; I was goin' crazy here. I can't stand these hills. I met Dick in a dance hall in Cripple Creek. He'd come in with the beef herd from the south. He told me about his little place. He was young an' decent. It looked like an out from the dance hall, an' I married him. An' the hell of it is he still thinks I'm on the up an' up. He's still in love with me.

"I tried. Honest, Smoky, I tried. But I'm no damn good an' it wasn't any use. We stayed most three years on this godforsaken place. An' he loves every bit of it. Horses an' cows is all he ever talks about, then cows an' horses again. I hate the lousy things. We were sittin' right here the night I blew my stack. I was thinkin' of bright lights an' music.

"'Hear 'em,' he says. 'Can't you hear 'em a-singin' from the rimrock?' Coyotes, they were, an' music to him. That's when I blew my stack.

"He didn't want to go to town an' work in the mine, he hated the lousy place. He went because of me, because I couldn't take it here. An' I loused the whole thing up. Smoothie owns most of the place now. An' it meant so much to Dick. . . . What'll I do, Smoky? If I run away, he'll follow me. Wherever I go, he'll come."

The big deputy shook his head. "I don't know what to say. I don't know what to tell you, I only wish I did." She was crying now. As the deputy wheeled his horse he spoke again, "I wish I knew, I only wish I knew."

She didn't see him go. She had slumped to the ground, her arms tight about her face, and her body was wracked as she sobbed.

B obby and Shorty were asleep in the little tepee when the storm broke. At the first sharp clap of thunder Bobby sat up in his blankets and stared wildly about, forgetting for the moment where he was. But as the thunder crashed again overhead he dived under the covers and pulled the tarp over his head.

Ever since he could remember he had been afraid of storms. The lightning terrified him. At home when it stormed in the night his mother always came into his room and sat by his bed. For somehow he couldn't help shaking. But he didn't want Shorty to find out that he was scared. He wondered how Shorty could sleep through anything like this for between crashes of thunder he could hear his regular breathing. It was a good thing they weren't sleeping together for he was shaking so hard he'd be bound to wake Shorty up. Presently he heard Shorty pull on his boots and go out of the tepee but he was only gone a moment.

"Somebody wrangles afoot in the morning," said Shorty, as he came back soaking wet. "One of the night horses has broke loose."

Bobby was shaking so he didn't care to answer for Shorty might find out. The rain was coming in torrents now. He could feel the water dripping in on him from a little hole in the tepee but he was too scared to move.

"Rain is what this country needs," said Shorty, pulling off his boots. Bobby didn't answer, he didn't trust himself to speak. By keeping his eyes closed tight and the tarp over his head he managed to shut out the blinding flashes. But at each clap of thunder he burrowed deeper into his bed.

It seemed an age to Bobby but presently the storm died away almost as suddenly as it came. He could still hear the rumble of distant thunder off toward the north. And he wondered if it was storming in town. He wasn't shaking now. He even tried to move from where the water dripped on him. And as the distant rumblings grew fainter he finally got up courage

enough to raise his head from out of the covers. It was dark in the little tepee but Shorty was snoring — gee, how he envied Shorty.

That had been a great day for Bobby, that day at Tin Cup Springs when the horse wrangler bowed up and quit after losing eight head of horses. For Shorty had cut him a mount of horses and given the job to him. Ever since he could remember he had spent a few weeks at the ranch and he had always ridden a gentle pony. But to be one of the outfit with a mount of horses all his own! Fingertail, Smoky, Scout, Old Rambler were all good horses too. And even if they didn't buck, Old Rambler could outrun Bill Jones' Paint.

It was nearly three weeks now since he'd been on the job and he hadn't lost a horse so far. By the time the outfit went to town for the Fourth of July rodeo he'd have forty dollars coming too. He didn't know how he'd spend quite all the money yet but one thing was sure, he'd get that pair of long-shanked, silver-mounted spurs in Charlie Collins' saddle shop. Mebbe he wouldn't strut! He even felt sorry for kids who lived in town and never got to ride a horse. He wouldn't trade places with anyone — if only it wouldn't storm.
. . .

It was still dark in the little tepee when old Sour Dough called "Chuck" next morning. As Bobby stirred drowsily in his blankets he could hear the low voices of the punchers who were drinking coffee by the fire. Presently he heard old Sour Dough's voice — "All twelve year old kids are sleepy-headed."

"I'll say he is," said Shorty, "he slept right through that storm last night."

He was glad that Shorty did not know, for the storm seemed like a bad dream now. He sat up in his blankets and rubbed his eyes. He would have liked to carry his clothes out by the fire to dress. He always did that when he was at home. And until that day at Tin Cup Springs he had always dressed by the fire in cow camp. But that was beneath his dignity now. So he slid into his levis and by the time he had finished pulling on his boots the first gray streaks of dawn were showing in the east.

Bobby never took his hat off when he washed his face in the morning, the water was too cold. And in cow camp there was no one to look behind his ears. He had coffee in cow camp too, as many cups as he liked. But best of all he liked the steak and hot biscuits. For Bobby was always hungry and old Sour Dough was a good cook, even if he was cranky at times and wouldn't let Bobby sit on the dutch-oven lid while he ate.

The punchers had all finished breakfast by the time Bobby filled his plate. But Pecos was still drinking coffee. Pecos never ate any breakfast. As Bobby stowed away the hot biscuits he wondered how Pecos could live on coffee and cigarettes and ride the rough string too.

Old Blue was the horse that had broken loose in the night. Bill Jones had wrangled alone. It was broad daylight when Bill came in sight with the remuda and Old Blue was the first horse down the trail to the water.

Evidently he'd gone back to the remuda in the night. Old Rambler came next and as the horses watered out, Bobby saw Fingertail, Smoky and Scout. Bill Jones hadn't had any breakfast yet. It was Pecos who took Bill's pony and drove the horses into the corral as soon as they had watered out.

"What horse do you want, kid?" asked Shorty, shaking out a little loop.

"Old Rambler," said Bobby. Shorty always caught the wrangler's horse first.

"Asia," said Bill Griggs as Shorty led Old Rambler out where Bobby slipped his bridle on.

"Slippers," yelled Bill Jones, who was still eating by the fire. And as Bobby was pulling up his latigo he heard Pecos ask for Tango. Unless ponies were caught napping they usually ducked and dodged. But once they felt the rope about their necks they were led out easily enough. But it took three punchers to drag Tango out to where Pecos' saddle lay.

Bobby would have liked to wait and see the fun, for Tango always bucked. But as soon as the last horse was caught up Shorty took down the corral bars and helped him turn the horses up the narrow trail to the big mesa. At the foot of the narrow trail Shorty pulled up his horse.

"You needn't bring 'em in at noon," he said, "for we won't want a change today. I'd graze 'em over toward Mud Springs an' throw 'em on the water about noon. Then if you're hungry, you can come on back to camp an' eat. We won't be back till late this evening."

Old Blue was always the first horse up the narrow trail. Old Blue was the leader of the remuda. About halfway up the trail he always stopped to blow. Everything stopped when Old Blue did. No amount of yelling on Bobby's part could make him move until he was ready. Everything below him he ignored completely unless the horses crowded him. Then he raised his head and flattened his ears and the horses would fall away on all sides to give him room. But Bobby wasn't in a hurry this morning and he let Old Blue take his time.

He was watching the big corral that lay far below him now. The punchers were all mounted except Pecos. And as Bobby watched he saw Pecos ease into the saddle and pull the blind. The next moment he saw Tango and Pecos go into the air together.

It was an old story to Bobby now but it always gave him a thrill to watch Pecos ease into the saddle and turn a wild one loose. The corral was so far below him he couldn't hear a sound but he knew that Tango was bawling. He always bawled when he bucked. And Pecos was using that heavy quirt. Boy — what a rider he was! It wouldn't be much longer now until Tango finally quit. Yep, Tango's head was up already for he didn't like that quirt. He was trotting around the corral and the punchers were riding out. As Pecos rode out he waved his hand and Bobby waved back to him.

The sun was almost an hour high before Bobby topped out with the last of the horses. From the top of the big mesa he could see for miles. From the rim of Mescal clear out beyond the Soda Hills, as far as he could see, there wasn't a cloud in the sky. The white

smoke was from the smelter in town. It was thirty
miles, he knew. The nine moving dots in the distance
was the outfit. He knew that Shorty was riding in the

lead and he tried to pick out Pecos. The distance was
too great, but he watched them until the moving dots
had crawled up the long limestone ridge and disappeared toward Haunted Canyon.

As the remuda grazed off across the big mesa,
Bobby made his first count. There was one horse miss-
ing, for there should be an even ninety head. Mebbe Six
X was gone, he caused more trouble than all the other
horses put together. He was always pulling out for
parts unknown. But presently Bobby located Six X,
who was grazing quietly in the middle of the herd.
Again he counted them and this time the count was
right.

For a time he practiced with his rope, but he grew tired of this and for want of something better to do he rode down to where the dead cow lay. The coyotes had been there since the rain. Their tracks were all about the place. Nearly every night they yelped about the camp; occasionally he saw one trotting off across the great flats. Once he had happened onto one that was only half-grown and he had chased him clear across the mesa. If he had only been riding Old Rambler that day instead of Scout he was sure he would have got a throw at him with his rope.

The horses were still grazing quietly. Bobby was on the point of riding back to them when he spotted a little bunch of cattle in the distance. They were moving slowly across the mesa toward the water at Mud Springs. Mebbe there was a long-eared calf in the bunch. As he kicked his pony into a gallop he took down his rope and shook out a little loop.

There were only two calves in the bunch but one was unbranded. As the cattle broke into a run he dug his heels into Old Rambler and went flying in their wake. Old Rambler was an old cow horse. There was no need to kick him for the game was old to him. As he flattened into a dead run the wind stung Bobby's face. The cattle were splitting up but the long-eared calf and one old cow were still running in the lead. Old Rambler was closing up the distance now at every jump and as the cow and long-eared calf turned sharply from him Bobby made his throw. But he missed the calf completely and caught the old cow by both horns. This was something he hadn't bargained for.

She was a big cow too. Well, there wasn't anything else to do but turn her loose. He'd seen the punchers do it lots of times. He reckoned he could too. But gee, he wished that Shorty was along. There wasn't a bush or tree in sight and she'd probably charge him when he turned her loose. He even thought of slipping the loop off the saddle horn. But if the punchers ever found he'd turned her loose with his rope on he'd never hear the last of it. No, that wouldn't do.

Old Rambler, old cow horse that he was, was keeping the rope tight. But as Bobby urged him toward her the old cow trotted off. Bobby put Old Rambler into a trot behind her and as the rope slacked off he flipped it over the cow's right hip just as he'd seen Shorty do. As the rope sagged almost to the ground he dug his heels into Old Rambler and put him into a run at the same time turning him sharply to the left.

Bobby came near losing his seat as Old Rambler hit the end of the rope. But he was off his horse the moment he saw the old cow hit the ground, working feverishly — the old cow might try to get up at any moment now. Slipping the old cow's tail between her legs and pulling it toward him with his left hand, at the same time putting all his weight against her back, he tugged at the loop around her horns. He couldn't budge the loop, however, for Old Rambler was holding on his end of the rope as hard as he knew how.

Then Bobby did as he'd seen Shorty do so many times before — jerking the rope twice sharply, he called to Old Rambler. Rambler, old cow horse that he was, moved up enough to give him slack. The old cow

was beginning to struggle but it was only the work of a moment now to slip the loop from off her horns and the moment the rope was free Bobby made a run for his horse.

Bobby was in the saddle coiling up his rope by the time the old cow regained his feet. If he had been on the ground the old cow would in all probability have

charged him. But she had had enough and trotted off toward the other cattle, shaking her head as she went. Bobby could still see the unbranded calf in the distance but he had had enough roping for one day too. So he rode slowly back to the horses.

The thunderheads were piling up. He hadn't noticed them before. There wasn't a cloud in sight when he reached the mesa that morning. But all about the rim of the horizon now the clouds were piling up. Gee, he hoped it wouldn't storm! It must be after ten o'clock, for he was getting hungry too. Well, it wouldn't be long until he watered the remuda out, then he'd go to camp and eat.

As he rode slowly around the horses he made his second count. Some of the horses were asleep. Old Blue always slept standing. But he counted twenty head that were stretched out on the ground. The sun made Bobby sleepy too and after riding slowly around the herd again he dismounted from Old Rambler and stretched out on the ground.

Bobby didn't know he'd been asleep but at the first low rumble of distant thunder he sat bolt upright and stared about. The air was deathly still. The sky was dark with heavy clouds and over toward Mescal the thunderheads were boiling now. Old Rambler was the only horse in sight. Which way had they gone? Mebbe they were on the water at Mud Springs, for it must be long past noon.

As Bobby swung into the saddle he dug his heels into Old Rambler and put him into a dead run. The other wrangler had gone to sleep and lost eight head.

But he had quit when Shorty offered to help him pack a horse and carry his bed along with him. Now what would Shorty say? For he'd gone to sleep and lost them all with a storm coming on! Why wouldn't Old Rambler run? Actually he was running now as fast as he knew how. But Bobby's heels still beat a tattoo against his ribs. If he only hadn't gone to sleep he'd be in camp with old Sour Dough right now. But if the horses were on the water at Mud Springs, mebbe he could make it yet before the storm broke. Why wouldn't Old Rambler run?

His heels were still drumming a tattoo against Old Rambler's ribs when he came in sight of the first horses and as he topped the little ridge above Mud Springs he set Old Rambler up, for the herd was grazing just below him.

He hadn't lost them after all. The horses had watered out and were grazing in little bunches all about the springs. But the storm was breaking over Mescal now, he couldn't see the rim. It was all of two miles back to camp but that wouldn't take him long. He was wheeling Old Rambler about for the run to camp when something in the distance caught his eye. Something moving toward Mescal — and his heart sank for he knew it was a horse.

Mebbe it wasn't his. But a quick count showed him he was one horse short and old Six X was gone. For the first time Bobby wished himself in town and the horses all in hell.

Yes, it was his horse all right, but let him go. Hadn't Shorty told him he could come to camp at noon? Shorty wouldn't know. He couldn't even see old Six X now for the storm was coming fast. It was only one horse, anyway, an' everyone was apt to lose a horse occasionally. But he hadn't lost a horse since he'd been on the job!

Bobby was crying and at each blinding flash he closed his eyes. But somehow he couldn't ride to camp and let old Six X go. The first big drops of rain were falling as he turned Old Rambler toward Mescal. Bobby was shaking too. At each blinding flash he closed his eyes. But he was one of the outfit and he urged Old Rambler on.

It was late that evening when the outfit rode into camp, but Bobby hadn't come. The punchers had dismounted and were gathered about the fire. Shorty and Pecos were on the point of riding out in search of him when Old Blue came into view.

"He probably lost a bunch today," said old Sour Dough, "for he never come in an' eat no bait at noon."

"I wouldn't blame him none if he'd lost 'em all," said Pecos, who was easing toward the coffeepot. "Lightnin' scares me to death an' he's nothin' but a kid."

But Shorty was making a silent count as the horses filed slowly down the narrow trail. Presently the last one of the horses came into view. It was old Six X and riding slowly at his heels was Bobby.

It was a tired and bedraggled Bobby who rode slowly down the trail that night. He was hungry too. But he wouldn't have traded places with anyone on earth. For he was one of the outfit and he knew that he'd made good.

OLD JIM NEWTON'S BOY

IT was just as Jimmy Newton had always planned. He had come back to ride. He had drawn a good horse, too. Old Hell Cat didn't try to take the chute apart when the punchers saddled him. Hell Cat was a wise old bucking horse. He was saving everything he had until the chute gate opened — then the big horse would explode.

Perched on the top rail of the chute, Jimmy waited his turn to come out. Yet the big horse in the chute below him had no part in Jimmy's thoughts.

It didn't seem like seven years. The place looked just the same. The old grandstand still looked as if it was ready to tumble down. As far back as he could remember it had always looked that way. There were a few new boards on the outfield fence in deep center. One of them was where that loose board used to be. That loose board had always been his entrance and his exit when he came to the ball park to play.

The little house on the hill above the park where he and Dad had lived still needed a coat of paint. Everything was just the same. Yet somehow everything was different, too. There were no familiar faces. Folks come and go in a mining camp. The little house stood empty now. It wasn't much of a place. Yet that little house had been home to him, the only one he had ever known.

His earliest recollections went back to that little house on the hill where he and Dad had lived. He couldn't remember his mother. Dad had been everything. From the time he was able to toddle he had always waited to meet his dad when he came off shift at the mine, he always sat at the brow of the hill where he could watch the trail below. Even when he was playing games with the kids in the ball park he didn't forget his dad. As soon as he was big enough to cook he always had supper ready, too, when Dad came home from work.

On Sundays they always sat together on the hill and watched the game below. The other kids shagged flies in the outfield during batting practice. But it was more fun to sit with Dad.

All the kids that hung about the ball park were going to be ball players, all except himself. He was always going to be a bronk rider like his dad had been as far back as he could remember.

It was the occasional Sundays when the cowboys came to the park to rope and ride that he got his biggest thrill. Dad knew them all. The ropers had never interested Jimmy like the boys who rode the buckers. There had been some good riders in that old ball park. There was Shep, and Shorty Caraway, Buff Edwards, Tom McKevitt and the rest. Sometimes a rider got away with something, an' fooled the crowd. But they never could fool his dad. He was always critical. It had to be just right.

It was always something to look forward to when

supper dishes were done. Dad told him stories then, stories of the open range and when the West was young. Stories of the Diamond A's in New Mexico. *There* was a regular spread! Dad had worked at the old Hash Knife outfit in Arizona too. That was where he rode ol' Cotton Eye, the famous bucking horse — rode him to a standstill an' spurred him every jump.

And there was that night when he waited on the hill for Dad that his small world fell apart. He had often thought of it since. Why couldn't it have been a bucking horse that killed his dad instead of the lousy mine? Neighbors had been kind. They had tried to take him in. But those days and nights that followed had been a nightmare. He had to run away!

He was twenty now. It didn't seem like seven years. He was a rider, too, just as his dad had been. Of course, he'd never be as good as Dad. But he'd been around. Prescott, Pendleton and Cheyenne — he knew them all. He'd finished in the money at the Garden, too. It had been an uphill pull. He never could have made the grade if it hadn't been for Dad; somehow Dad was always back of him and watching when he forked a bucking horse.

He had started out wrangling horses, the way they all began; roping and reading brands and earmarks had come easy to him, too. It was funny how the things he wanted most had always been so hard.

He had learned to ride by countless falls, the way they all began. But he never could have made the grade without his dad. No, he'd never be the rider that his dad had been no matter how he tried.

"Hey, you, on the chute — wake up!" A puncher was grinning up at him. "You're comin' out right away." Then he heard his own name called.

"Jimmy Newton on Hell Cat. Riding out of chute number four."

As he eased himself into the saddle and felt for his stirrups a quiver ran through the big horse, it was like an electric shock. Jimmy adjusted the rope again, he had it a little short. He set himself to meet the first big jolt, nodded his head, and then the chute gate opened.

For an instant Hell Cat blinked at the ground. Then he was no longer a horse. Jimmy was riding eleven hundred pounds of dynamite wrapped up in a bit of black hide.

Of all the horses he had ever rode, Hell Cat was the worst. He knew it before the bawling horse had

made three jumps with him. But Jimmy knew no horse
that ever lived could buck him off right then. It was as
if someone else was riding. He had no part in it. He and
Dad were watching the ride again from the hill above
the park.

The pick-up man was alongside now. Hell Cat's
head was up. Jimmy hadn't heard the gun, but he gave
pick-up the rein. Pick-up's arm was around him. He
was on the ground again. For an instant he wobbled on
his pins until his head had cleared.

He didn't hear the roaring crowd, his ears were
pounding so. But he knew it was the best ride he had
ever made. He had spurred the big horse from shoulder
to rump from the time the chute gate opened until Hell
Cat's head came up. He hadn't made a bobble. Dad
couldn't have picked a flaw.

The old-timer had walked to meet him. "You old
Jim Newton's boy?"

Jimmy nodded his head and smiled. "You knew
my dad?"

"I knew your dad right well, I used to work with
him back at the Diamond A's. You favor ol' Jim, too,
that is, you look like him. You made a nice ride, son."

Jimmy would have liked him to stay an' talk, but
the old-timer had turned away.

Back in the grandstand the old-timer was seated
with another of his kind. "It was ol' Jim Newton's boy.
Somehow I can't believe it yet. I never saw a better ride
than that kid made today. An' ol' Jim, his dad, was always plumb helpless on a horse. Poor ol' Jim, he
couldn't ride in a wagon."

MAN AND HORSE

Some horses like some men have stouter hearts than others of their kind. They go until they fall. They are the great-hearted horses that ask no odds. Ponies that don't know what it means to quit. Jack Freckles was that kind.

Jack Freckles was all horse. He spent most of his life in the rough string. The big horse was an outlaw. Jack Freckles always bucked. If the man aboard was a rider the big horse sensed it too. Often he would go for days on end without a kink in his back. The horse was only waiting for his chance to catch his rider off guard. When the rider least expected it the big horse would explode. Once the rider was on the ground the horse would snap like a loafer wolf and strike with both forefeet. Jack Freckles was a killer. The big horse hated men.

There were plenty of peelers who came to the ranch who could ride the big freckled horse in the corral but to get out on the range an' really work on him was something else again. If Jack Freckles had been with a rodeo he would no doubt have made a name as a famous bucking horse. Since the outfit was working cattle he didn't earn his salt. He wasn't worth a dime to the outfit until Klink came to work at the ranch.

Klink drifted in from nowhere an' worked a year with us. We knew no more about him when he left than we did the day he came. He was on the slim side with smoky-colored eyes. He was all man too. The outfit would have liked him if he'd given us a chance. In all the time he was around he didn't speak a dozen words to anyone that wasn't necessary. He kept strictly to himself. It was the way he had with horses that interested us.

He knew a horse inside an' out as few men do. There was some sort of an understanding between the brooding, silent cowboy and the freckled outlaw horse we never could figure out. We said it was because the two were much alike. It wasn't until a long time after Klink had quit an' drifted on that we came to realize just how much alike they were.

Horses are like humans when it comes to certain things. Whenever you find a spoiled or outlaw horse there's a reason back of it all. Sometimes, of course, it's plain cussedness. But usually when a horse goes bad some cowboy is at fault.

Jack Freckles' early life was that of any range colt. His mammy was a wild range mare. The colt had his daddy's looks. He was a big freckled stud that ran with his bunch of mares an' colts on the roughest part of the range. They ranged from the big river to a spring underneath the rim. Keeping to the pines and juniper in summer and coming down with the first big snow. No other place is ever really home to a horse except the place where he is foaled. Whenever Jack Freckles was turned loose at the ranch he always headed back.

Except for an occasional rider on the skyline Jack Freckles had never seen a man until he was six months old. They were grazing on the edge of the mesa that day when the old stud gave the alarm. Two riders were swooping down on them as fast as their ponies could run. As Jack Freckles raced beside his mother other riders began to close in. The whole band was hazed into a big corral where the little colts were gelded and branded.

The colt was probably too spooked that day to feel the burn from the searing iron. But the little colt's first contact with any man was something he never forgot.

The spring Jack Freckles was four years old marked the end of his real freedom. The big colt had never been corraled since the day that he was gelded. As the riders swooped down on him again Jack Freckles ran for his life. He easily outran every other horse in the herd that the riders had hazed together but the odds were all against him. Each way the big colt turned he found his way to freedom cut off. The riders were closing in. Jack Freckles was swept into the horse corral along with the rest of the herd before he knew just what had happened.

It is as natural for a bronk to buck as it is for a pig to grunt. Most of them gradually give it up when they finally learn that they can't unseat the rider. It is usually after the first few saddles that the real temperament of a pony begins to show itself. Some quit bucking after the first few rides and give no further trouble. Others respect the quirt. But there are always a few who fight their worst whenever it is used.

Flint Jones was breaking horses at the ranch that spring. Flint was a rider, too, or he wouldn't have had the job. But Flint was far more interested in how well he rode than in what he taught a horse.

Jack Freckles was quick and willing to learn. After the first few saddles he quit striking when Flint approached his head. He was quick to learn the feel of the rein on his neck, the big colt could turn on a dime. He still pitched each time he was saddled or when some little thing went wrong. But there was nothing vicious about him. It was his way of letting off steam. If Flint had gone a little slower Jack Freckles would have eventually quit pitching and become a good cow horse. Flint made his big mistake with the colt when he used the quirt on him.

They had it out one morning on the big flat outside the corral. Flint tried to whip it out of him when Jack Freckles bucked that morning. Each jump the big colt made with him Flint swung that heavy quirt. And Jack Freckles bucked that morning as he had never bucked before. Each time he felt the heavy quirt Jack Freckles fought back, bawling like a maddened steer. Long, bloody welts began to appear on the big colt's heaving flanks. And there was blood on the big colt's shoulders where Flint raked him with his spurs. Flint Jones was a rider or he couldn't have kept his seat. But the big, freckled colt was game. He gave everything he had that morning. He pitched until he fell.

That ride on the flat in front of the corral marked the change in the big colt's life. Flint never tried to whip him again but Jack Freckles never forgot. Every man was the big colt's enemy now. He snapped and

struck at anyone who dared come near his head.

Each time Flint rode him after that the colt was harder to ride. It isn't until a bronk has been bucking a while that he learns the real trick of it. It was when the big colt finally learned that he couldn't unseat Flint that he began to use his head. He played a waiting game.

One morning for the first time since he had been rode there was no kink in the big colt's back. Jack Freckles didn't hang his head and pitch when the cowboy topped him off. He trotted off that morning like any old cow horse.

It was a long drive to the river that day. There was no change of horses at noon. Horses and men were all dead tired when they got into the ranch that night. The big colt was dog tired too. But he was not too tired to overlook the thing he was waiting for.

They were coming through the big corral gate at the home ranch when the big colt saw his chance. Flint had turned in his saddle casually to speak to a rider behind him. Feeling his rider off balance Jack Freckles hung his head. Loosened by the unexpected jump of the colt Flint never regained his seat.

It was what the big colt had waited for. He was on Flint like a flash, snapping at him like a wolf, striking with both forefeet. Luckily for Flint the riders were close. They drove Freckles off and carried Flint into the house. The fall work was over before Flint could ride again.

Other peelers came an' went. The broncs that were broke with Jack Freckles that spring were good cow horses now. Each spring and fall when the work began Jack Freckles was caught up. He was bigger and stronger than ever. He was meaner too as the years went slipping by. He snapped an' struck at everyone. The big horse had never forgotten.

It took a real rider to ride him now even in the corral. If the rider used a quirt on him he bucked until he fell. And bucking had become an art with him, the big horse knew every trick. Once he loosened the rider an inch the rider never got it back.

To get out on the range an' really work on him was something out of the question. Sooner or later the big horse would catch his rider off guard. Some little thing would go wrong. Anyway they figured him he would pull the unexpected. He wasn't worth two bits at best as far as the outfit went. Yet there wasn't a man among us but admired his fighting heart.

Klink drifted into the ranch one night just before the fall work started. Except for a rough-string rider the outfit was full handed.

Jack Freckles had become a sort of a trial horse when a new peeler drifted in. If a man could ride the big outlaw he could ride most anything. Next morning when the nighthawk drove the ponies in Klink roped the freckled horse.

If there was anything between them they didn't show it then. Jack Freckles struck with both forefeet when Klink went down the line. When Klink had laced his saddle on an' stepped across, Jack Freckles bogged his head. And the big horse never bucked any harder in his whole life than he did that morning with Klink. And Klink took everything Jack Freckles gave. The man was a riding fool.

Klink was warned that the big horse would bide his time and catch him off his guard. "We'll get along," he said. We didn't realize at the time what a speech it was for him. A yes or no with any of us was as far as he ever went. When he could make himself understood by nodding his head he didn't bother to speak.

But he and Jack Freckles got along, just as he said

they would. After that first morning in the corral Jack
Freckles didn't buck. And we noticed after the first few
saddles the big horse had quit snapping and striking at
him when Klink approached his head. What's more,
the big cowboy did the work of a regular hand on the
freckled outlaw horse.

Jack Freckles knew better than any of us how
well Klink could ride. But there had been other good
riders too. Sooner or later they all let down or got care-
less in some way. And there had been other times when
the big horse had gone for days on end without a kink
in his back. When Jack Freckles was acting his best was
always the time to watch him most.

Klink had been with the outfit a month when Jack
Freckles' big chance came. The outfit was working on
Rock Creek that day, rounding up wild cattle. Klink
was at the hold-up when one of the big steers broke out.
Unable to turn the critter the puncher took down his
rope.

The cowboy made a clean throw catching the
steer by the horns. It was when Klink set Jack Freckles
up that the hondoo broke. It caught the cowboy
squarely between the eyes when the rope snapped
back, knocking him off his horse.

Jack Freckles' chance had finally come. His rider
lay stunned on the ground at his feet. There were no
riders close enough to drive the big killer away. Yet the
horse did not snap an' strike as he had so often done
before. Nor did he break to run. The big outlaw never
moved in his tracks although he trembled from head to
foot.

It was then that Jack Freckles did a strange thing,
unbelievable for him. He touched the man on the
ground with his nose. He nuzzled his fallen rider. It was
only when other riders rode up that the big killer flattened his ears. They kept their distance too while the
big horse stood his ground. Not until Klink was on his
feet again would he let anyone come near.

Just what was between the man and horse we never
understood and none of the outfit ever learned how it
had come about. As far as we could see Klink treated
all of his horses alike. He didn't make pets of any of
them, Klink didn't ride that kind. Although we did
hear him talk to Jack Freckles sometimes when they
were alone together.

The big, smoky-eyed puncher preferred horses to
men. He didn't trust his own kind. Even about the
camp at night he was as watchful as a cat. When a stray
rider occasionally drifted in Klink was always the first
to hear him. The big puncher would be up and moving
about long before the rider got in.

We didn't care two hoots in hell what he had done
or what he was wanted for. It was none of our affair.
There had been other riders at the outfit whose con-
science was none too clear. Given a little time they always softened a bit when they were among their own
kind. But the slim, smoky-eyed puncher never let down
from the time he rode into the ranch until the day he
rode away. You could no more get familiar with him
than with the outlaw horse he rode.

He never went to town with the outfit in the year
he worked at the ranch. When he caught Jack Freckles

up occasionally at night an' rode away alone he was
always back at daybreak. Later we learned from punchers who had seen the horse that Klink had been in town.
While Jack Freckles waited at the rack for him the big
cowboy drank alone.

He range-branded on Rock Creek that winter and
camped by himself on the roughest part of the range.
He fed two horses grain. One, of course, was Jack
Freckles. His other mount was a big black that had
never been out of the rough string. Occasionally when
a puncher came in from his line camp for chuck he
would jokingly ask how the outlaws were making out.
Klink caught more steers that winter than any man on
the range.

While Klink broke horses that spring and summer
at the home ranch Jack Freckles was turned out to rest.
It wasn't until the fall work started that he was caught
up again. Naturally the outfit was curious as to how the
big freckled horse would act with Klink after months
on the open range.

Klink roped his string of rough ones out. He was
to ride twelve head that work. All of us were watching
when it came Jack Freckles' turn. As Klink walked
slowly toward him the big outlaw slung his head. As
Klink approached Jack Freckles' ears went back, the
big horse wasn't certain. It was then Klink stopped an'
spoke to him and slowly Jack Freckles came.

At intervals the big horse stopped, yet each time he
came on until Klink could have touched the big horse
with his hand, yet the cowboy made no move. As the
big horse stood facing the cowboy, he trembled from

head to foot. It was when Klink spoke to him again
that he nuzzled his smoky-eyed rider.

It was the custom when an old hand left the outfit
to give the waddie a horse. He could pick any one in
his string. The Old Man was at the corral that day.
While Klink had only worked a year he gave the horse
to him.

"Any time you leave," he said, "the freckled horse
is yours."

But Klink was not riding Jack Freckles the day he
rode away.

Steer Mountain was the biggest drive on the lower
range. It was hard on any horse. Unless a puncher
picked his toughest one he was apt to come in afoot.
Klink picked Jack Freckles that morning as he was
riding outside circle. He had the longest ride. There
were three of us at the hold-up. The rest went on the
drive. We had waited all of three hours before the cattle began to come down. Everything had started well.
The drive was running smooth. The first cattle had
reached the hold-up. Others were coming in when a
band of wild horses that had been jumped on the drive
began to ball things up.

As the wild bunch went racing through them, cattle that were coming down began to rim out an' turn
back. The band of wild horses had split up now, they
were running in all directions. One bunch of big steers
was turned back an' headed down a long ridge. If they
reached the saddle on Sycamore we would lose every
one in the bunch. Tommy Turner had seen them, he was
racing to cut them off. But Tommy couldn't overtake

them. Tommy's pony was through. As we watched
him pull up his tired horse another rider appeared.
Klink was coming down through the short chops as fast
as Jack Freckles could run.

It was too much to expect of any horse. Klink had
started his race too late. But as they raced down through
the broken short chops the big horse began to creep up.
Few horses could have kept their feet on such rough
and broken ground. Yet Jack Freckles kept his stride.
Once when they were out of sight we thought the horse
had fallen. But Jack Freckles was running smoothly
when they reached the open ridge.

It was when they reached the long ridge that the
big horse began to gain. He was eating up the distance
now with every stride he took. Jack Freckles already
had a long ride back of him that morning on the roughest part of the range. Yet Klink used no quirt or spur
an' if he spoke we couldn't hear. What a horse he was!

If the big horse had only shown some sign that he
was hurt Klink would have pulled him up. Not for all
the steers in the world would he have hurt the freckled
horse. And Jack Freckles gave no outward sign that he
was breaking his gallant heart. Klink wanted him to
run, he kept his unbroken stride.

And Jack Freckles won his race that day. The cattle were headed an' turned. Only then did his great
heart quit. Klink had pulled the big horse up. As we
watched, Jack Freckles stumbled. Then the big horse
went to his knees.

It was all over when we rode up. Jack Freckles had

run his last race. As Klink held the big horse's head in his arms he cried like a little kid.

Klink didn't stay long after that. He quit an' drifted on. We didn't know where he went. What's more he didn't bother to tell anyone "So long" the morning he pulled out. But the big, smoky-eyed puncher isn't the kind that is easily forgotten.

We were camped at Sycamore one night when an old waddie drifted in. The old man was a northern puncher who had known Klink as a boy. The old man had known his people too. Upstanding an' fine they were an' Klink had always been a friendly kid until this mix-up came. When the old man spoke a lot of things we never had understood were simpler to us, why the big puncher preferred horses to men was easy to understand. And we knew what was eatin' the smoky-eyed Klink on those nights alone by the fire.

The old-timer wouldn't tell us Klink's real name or just what the trouble was. But he did say that three men had been involved and that Klink had been made the goat. On the testimony of the other two they convicted him. And Klink had served his time. He had served eight years in a northern penitentiary where he had brooded all the while. When they turned him out Klink killed both men and made his getaway.

We often wondered where he was as the months went slipping by. At nights round the fire when the talk was of horses an' men some waddie was always sure to speak of the smoky-eyed Klink and the big freckled horse he had rode. But it wasn't until Dick

Wilson came to work with us that we got the rest of the story.

After Klink left the ranch he had gone to work for an outfit in the north. Dick had worked with him there. They had range-branded together that winter an' slept in the same tepee. Dick was the kid of the outfit. He worshiped the smoky-eyed puncher. No one he had ever known could rope or ride with him.

Although Klink seldom spoke Dick knew from little things the big puncher did that he was fond of him. Dick was always sleepy headed, Klink had to waken him. Often he would have the horses wrangled and the breakfast cooked before he turned Dick out. And once the big puncher had spoken when he woke Dick up that morning: "Kid, you want to always sleep like that. Once I could sleep myself."

They had moved back into headquarters. They were range-branding under the mountain the day the big storm came. The weather was warm and sunny when they left the ranch that morning. By ten o'clock the sky was overcast. The warmth of the early morning had turned to bitter cold.

As they headed back to headquarters it started spitting snow. It was when they reached the open flats that they got the full force of the storm. They were the last two punchers in. The house was snug and warm as they listened to the roar of the wind outside and the hiss of the driving snow.

"Let 'er storm," said Old Scotty, the foreman. He was in mighty good humor now that all of his men were in. The punchers had started a stud game when something bumped into the house. For a moment they thought it was a steer confused by the storm. It was a man at the door.

He was a nester who lived just a few miles south. He was in pretty bad shape. When they finally brought him round where he could speak he said that one of his kids was very sick. His woman wanted a doctor.

Everyone knew it was hopeless, it was twenty miles to town. It was too much to expect any man to face the storm that day. "There's not a chance in the world," said the foreman. Several cowhands nodded their heads. Klink must have known it was hopeless too. But he got into his heavy clothes and without a word or as much as a glance behind he walked into the storm.

Dick followed him to the saddle shed. Klink wouldn't let him go but Dick rode with two of the punchers when they took the nester home.

It was daybreak when they got back to the ranch and bitter cold. But the storm had spent itself and the little nester kid had pulled through the night without the aid of a doctor. They were riding into the saddle shed when they found Klink's saddled horse. The horse had come in some time in the night but there was no sign of the smoky-eyed rider.

The whole outfit rode that morning. There were no tracks on the snow-covered ground. They knew Klink had taken the trail to town; the outfit rode that way. It wasn't until the trail ran through the cedar brakes that the punchers struck his sign.

Here the trail was somewhat sheltered from the

wind an' driving snow. The sign told everything. To
the punchers the story was just as plain as if it was written down. Here Klink had dismounted. He was walking to keep warm. Now he was back on his horse again.
His pony wanted to quit. The horse had wheeled from
the trail an' turned into a thicket when Klink roweled
him with the spurs. It was when they reached the end
of the cedar brake that the pony had quit on him.

The horse had refused to face the storm across the
wind-swept flats. Klink was walking an' leading again.
Here he had turned the pony loose an' gone ahead
afoot. A mile or so further on they struck his sign
where the trail was protected again. Klink was weaving now as he walked. Here he had fallen for the first
time but he had got to his feet an' fought his way ahead.
It was just a little further on that they found him. He
was lying face down in the snow.

Knowing every trick of the range as he did, it
would have been a simple thing for the big puncher to
have taken shelter in a thicket an' built himself a fire.
It had probably never entered his head. Like the big
freckled horse he had rode at the ranch, he would go
until he fell.

We realized now just how much in common there
was between the freckled, outlaw horse and the big,
smoky-eyed cowboy. How much alike they were. He
was all horse, Jack Freckles. Klink was all man too.

WITH BATED BREATH

I DIDN'T want any trouble. The girl didn't mean anything to either of us. I had only danced with her twice. Mason had been in the valley a year. I only knew him by sight. When Mason told me to lay off I thought the man was joking until I saw his face.

The thing had happened so quick it was hard to get it all straight. There was only room in the school house for six couples to dance. There was a fire going outside the door. There was probably a dozen punchers around the fire when Mason jumped me out.

No one had ever rode me before. I didn't know what to do. When I tried to pass it off as a joke it only made things worse. I was nineteen years old an' husky but I'd never been in a fight. I could feel myself shaking all over.

I'd never felt so helpless in my life. When he cussed me I started to bawl. I was turning to walk away from the fire when he slapped me across the mouth. Some of the punchers were snickering. Mason was snickering too. All I could see was Mason's face. Everything else was a blur. I knew I was playing right into his hands when I swung at him but I couldn't stand it no longer.

It wasn't until I was halfway back to the ranch

that things began to get clear. Mason had said he would kill me the next time we met up. It was funny how I could remember that when everything else was so hazy but the words seemed to burn in my head.

It was breaking light when I stopped at Oak Creek. I felt sick all over then. It was all I could do to get down from my horse but I knew the cold water would help. I didn't feel anything during the fight. Now I could hardly walk.

We had evidently rolled into the fire. I could see that my clothes had been burned. Two .30-30 shells in my pocket were bent. Then I remembered he had give me the boots the last time I was down. A puncher had helped me onto my horse. I didn't know who he was. That was after Mason had said he would kill me the next time we met up.

I knew I couldn't go through with a gun fight. If I stayed that's what it meant. I'd seen Carter kill Johnson when I was a kid. The thought of it still made me sick. I didn't want any trouble. There was nothing to do but pull out.

I told the Ole Man what had happened when I got into the ranch. I told him I was leaving until the thing blowed over. He had taken me in when the folks died. I'd been with him since I was a kid but when the Ole Man finally spoke I wouldn't have known his voice.

"So you figger on leaving the valley until the thing blows over?" His voice cut like a knife. "Well, you might as well figger on leaving for good. If Mason don't run you off when you come back, somebody else will."

The Ole Man avoided me all that day. At supper he didn't speak. In the evenings we always set an' talked for a spell. For the first time since I had lived with him the Ole Man went to bed without a word to me.

I couldn't sleep. It was the worst night I ever put in. I knew I'd let the Ole Man down. That was the thing that hurt. I didn't want to leave the valley. I couldn't go through with a gun fight. Nothing seemed to make sense.

I couldn't keep Carter an' Johnson out of my head. No matter how hard I tried. I could see the thing all over as if it happened that day — the way Johnson looked when Carter shot him down, the look in Carter's face as he stood over him an' pumped shell after shell into Johnson as he lay on the ground. But the thing that bothered me most of all was the way the Ole Man had looked at me. I'd let the Ole Man down.

The Ole Man had given me an ole "45" six-shooter years before that I always kept in my bed. I never had packed the thing. By the half-light from the window I cleaned an' oiled the gun. Then I cleaned my .30-30 an' tiptoed out of the house. When I wrangled the ponies that morning I saddled the best horse in my string. We were supposed to go to the U Bars that day an' get some of our cattle they'd gathered. It was the outfit where Mason worked. I figgered I might as well get it over with as long as it had to be.

The Ole Man had breakfast ready when I came into the house. We didn't speak all through the meal. It wasn't until he had caught up his horse that I said I was going with him. His face was always hard as flint.

But when he spoke it was the voice I'd always known.

"I won't ask you to go today," he says, "you know Mason is working there. But I knew you wouldn't run away, Johnny Boy, you belong in the valley, son."

When I said I figgered on going along the Ole Man went into the house an' got his .30-30. Before he slung on the gun he pumped the shells out of the magazine into his hat. He worked the lever fast. He wiped each shell off carefully before he slipped it back into the gun. I took a last look at the ranch after we swung up. I didn't figger to see it again.

We were within a mile of the U Bar camp when the Ole Man pulled up his horse. "I wish I could take

this off your hands — I wish I could," he says. His voice
was quiet an' gentle. "It's up to Mason to make the first
move. It's him that's made all the talk."

The Ole Man was speaking again — "Keep cool
an' don't get excited no matter what the man says.
Don't pull your gun till you're ready to shoot — when
you pull it, come shootin', son. Get a slug into Mason's
belly, don't think of anything else. If Mason pulls any
kind of a crooked move I'll kill the bastard myself."

I couldn't trust myself to speak, I could only nod
my head.

The U Bar cook was in camp alone. Dinner was
almost ready. He said the outfit was branding out at a

corral just up the canyon. We didn't ride two hundred
yards till we met them coming in. The outfit was making a beanpot race. The punchers were running their
horses. We pulled our horses out of the trail. Most of
the punchers spoke as they passed us. When several of
them looked behind we knew that Mason was coming.

Mason was riding a big black horse. He was coming at a gallop. At sight of us he tried to pull the big
black up but the big horse fought for his head. He was
still fighting his head when he passed us an' Mason
yelled "Hello." Me an' the Ole Man nodded, then
Mason yelled "Hello" again as if we hadn't heard him.

When he finally pulled the big horse down we
followed him into camp. I could see the butt of his six-
shooter underneath the batwinged chaps. The scabbard
was built into the leggins where it was protected by the
flap. It was a common way of packing a gun when a
man was on a horse. A man could reach it quick. The
flap protected it from the heavy brush. An' there was
another advantage, it couldn't be seen from the front.
When Mason dismounted from his horse he took his
leggins off an' he pitched the leggins, gun an' all, on the
ground just out of camp. The gesture was obviously
peaceful. He knew we'd seen the gun.

We rode to the other side of camp. When the Ole
Man got down from his horse he pulled his .30-30 from
the scabbard an' leaned it against a tree. The Ole Man
parked himself on his heels right beside the gun. He got
out his pipe an' filled it, then he told me to go an' eat.
I sat beside the Ole Man after I filled my plate. When
I finished I put my things in the roundup pan. Then I

parked beside the rifle while the Ole Man got his bait.

There was the usual roundup talk that goes with a meal in camp. Tom Nash, the foreman, told the Ole Man they had gathered thirty head of our stuff. The Ole Man spoke of a U Bar saddle horse that he had seen not over a week before that was running with the wild bunch.

One of the men attempted a joke. It was a pretty feeble effort. Bill Jones, who was just my age, laughed so loud that several of the punchers turned an' looked at him. Bill's face turned scarlet then. Nothing about the meal seemed real to me. I could feel the Ole Man's presence above everything else in camp. Never in all the years I'd lived with him had the Ole Man seemed so close.

I was conscious of trifling things I wouldn't have noticed before. The cook had shaved that morning. I counted three little cuts on his cheek. There was a little mole on Dick Smith's right hand. Dick had often stayed all night at the ranch. I'd never seen it before.

Mason avoided me with his eyes. His face was the color of ashes. He didn't speak all through the meal. I tried to keep Carter an' Johnson out of my head. I kept looking at his belt buckle, thinking of what the Ole Man had said. "Get a slug into his belly, don't think of anything else." I wondered if I could go through with it when the blow-off finally come.

I watched Mason pull on his batwinged chaps an' swing onto his big black horse. He rode just behind the foreman. As soon as the men were mounted we followed them to the corral. The Ole Man told me to hold

the "cut." It put me off by myself. Occasionally I'd get
a flash of Mason through the dust. But he didn't come
anywhere close. I'll never forget the relief I felt when I
saw the Ole Man coming an' we started the cattle for
home.

The valley had never looked so good before. I
didn't have to leave! The Ole Man an' I sat late that
night. He spoke about my folks. He said my dad had
never took things laying down. He always seen it
through. I told the Ole Man I couldn't have faced it out
if it hadn't been for him. But the Ole Man only shook
his head.

"You belong in the valley, Johnny Boy," he says,
"you belong in the valley, son."

I thought it was all over. But it wasn't over. The blow-off came a month later. I'd gone into town alone. I'd gone in to another dance. I got a room in the hotel to change clothes. My room was just off the bar. I was shaving when I heard voices at the bar. Something went all over me. I put down my razor an' listened. It was Mason's voice. He was talking to the bartender.

"With that ole musk-hog sitting by his rifle I didn't have a chance the other day in camp. Jackson's alone tonight."

The bartender said something. I couldn't make it out. I tried to finish shaving. I cut myself twice on the cheek. I finally got so nervous I put the razor down. Mason was speaking again:

"I spose I'll have to get the Ole Man later but I aim to kill Jackson tonight."

I couldn't stand it no longer. The six-shooter the Ole Man had given me was laying on the bed. I cocked the gun an' held it in the waistband of my pants. I didn't even wipe the lather off my face. Mason was still talking as I came through the door.

Mason's back was toward me. He could see me in the mirror that stood behind the bar. In the mirror I could see his gun. It was in his waistband where he could get it quick.

Mason made no move to turn. His hand slid toward his gun. I couldn't shoot him in the back — I was thinking of Ole Johnson. I watched him pull the gun. He pulled it slow. An' still he made no move to turn. Then he slid the gun across the bar. He put his head down on his arm an' cried like a little kid.

I couldn't speak. When Mason finally raised his head I pointed to the door. I never saw him again.

The bartender stood beside me. He shook my hand. He said I needed a drink. But I didn't want a drink. I wanted to be alone.

I walked into my room an' laid down on the bed. It was all I could do to make it. I felt weak an' sick all over. I didn't want any trouble.